MW00804039

FURY OF THE ORCAS

HUNTER SHEA

SEVERED PRESS
HOBART TASMANIA

FURY OF THE ORCAS

Copyright © 2017 Hunter Shea
Copyright © 2017 by Severed Press

WWW.SEVEREDPRESS.COM

All rights reserved. No part of this book may be
reproduced or transmitted in any form or by any
electronic or mechanical means, including
photocopying, recording or by any information and
retrieval system, without the written permission of
the publisher and author, except where permitted by law.
This novel is a work of fiction. Names,
characters, places and incidents are the product of
the author's imagination, or are used fictitiously.
Any resemblance to actual events, locales or persons,
living or dead, is purely coincidental.

ISBN: 978-1-925711-43-1

All rights reserved.

This one's for Rich Duncan. Thank you for everything, and I do mean everything.

"They are no longer really orcas but mutants, genetically killer whales but made up of warped psychologies."

— John Hargrove, Beneath the Surface: Killer Whales, SeaWorld, and the Truth Beyond Blackfish

CHAPTER ONE

Chet Clarke both hated and loved his job.

"Why is he doing that?" the boy with the face of a wizened old man said, palms flat against the Plexiglas shield. His voice was high and reedy, like he'd taken a hit from a helium balloon.

The sun fried the back of Chet's neck to a crisp as he stared down at the manic orca. It flipped around several times before ramming its head into the side of the tank.

"It's a she," Chet said, hands balled into fists. He kept them shoved deep in his pockets so no one could see.

"Taka sounds like a boy's name," the kid said, his unblinking, bulging eyes glued to the spectacle.

Chet did everything he could not to start shouting at the staff that milled around the tank. Why the hell was this kid still here? He shouldn't be seeing this. Not unless they wanted to make sure he had nightmares for the rest of his short life.

"Do you think she's mad because she's hungry?"

Chet looked to Rosario Benitez for some help. He locked onto her wide, dark brown eyes, begging her to shuffle the kid away before he lost his temper.

Rosario had been a trainer at the Anaheim Dolphinarium for seven years. She was very good at what she did, despite having one of the most loathsome professions Chet could think of. She loved the orcas and treated them as best she could. But they were still wild beasts locked in tanks that were a mere drop in the vast ocean they should be traversing.

The orca's massive dorsal fin was bent over on itself, flopping from side to side as she rocketed around the tank.

"Taka's just playing around. She gets like that when she's tired," she said, draping her arm over the kid's shoulder and leading him away from the observation platform above the tank.

"Is she going to hurt herself?"

Chet had overheard one of the trainers say the kid had Progeria. The disease made him look as if he'd rapidly aged, his small frame and bulbous head seeming so fragile, Chet worried about accidentally bumping into him as he assessed the situation. The boy had been given a special behind the scenes look into the orca show thanks to a gift from the Dreams Come True Association.

Chet was pretty sure this wasn't the magic moment the charity had intended for the terminal boy.

Rosario was quick on her feet. She assured him, "Killer whales have extremely thick skulls. They have to in order to take down big whales and sharks. Taka doesn't even feel it. It's just the same as how they can't feel the cold temperatures when they migrate up to Alaska. Nature designed them to be tough customers."

Taka took another crack at braining herself, this time right below Chet's feet. He felt the impact in his molars.

The platform reverberated, a bucket of half frozen fish toppling over. Chet skipped over one of the fish as it slid past him, bouncing off the Plexiglas.

This time, there was blood in the water.

"Hand me another," Chet snapped at the trainer standing by the bucket. It took him a moment to close his mouth and realize Chet was talking to him. He fumbled around to grab hold of one of the slippery fish.

Tossing it in the water, Chet watched as it sunk to the bottom of the tank. Taka gave it a brief glance and swam away.

"Dammit," Chet hissed.

The first dose of Valium wasn't working and if Taka wasn't going to eat the fish he'd dosed with the drug, he'd have to resort to the tranquilizer gun. He hated to use it and always kept it as an absolute last resort.

This wasn't the first time Taka had exhibited this behavior. She was getting worse and worse. He'd seen it in almost every orca he treated at marine parks all around the world. Even a captive born orca like Taka, who never knew true freedom, wanted to be out of its confined home.

Orcas committing acts to harm themselves was nothing new. If people knew how many actually killed themselves, either when they were captured in the wild or later when a switch went off in their minds that enough was enough, Chet was sure all orca shows would shut down overnight.

Who was he fooling? Even after that documentary came out, exposing the ugly truth behind the mad notion of keeping orcas in captivity, they still flocked to the shows in droves.

Either they were willfully ignorant or just plain stupid. Chet would put all his chips on the latter.

"She's bleeding," the kid said, pulling away from Rosario to press his ancient face against the glass.

"Kid, you need to get back," Chet said, waving him away.

Taka swam in circles, a stream of blood billowing from her crown like smoke from a skywriting plane.

"I thought you said she was playing," the boy said, turning to Rosario.

"She'll be fine," Rosario said with a faltering smile. She flicked a glance at Chet. He gave an almost imperceptible shake of his head. Taka was not going to be fine. Not today. Not ever. Orcas didn't magically get better, not when their minds had gone.

With a great rush of water, Taka broke the surface.

The trainers screamed.

The little boy stared at Taka's sleek black and white body, gleaming in the oppressive sun, as she arced above the tank.

Chet's heart froze.

No!

There was no time to worry if the boy's skeletal frame could hold up under his touch. Chet dashed to his left, scooping the boy in one arm and grabbing Rosario with his free hand. He left his feet, diving for safety as the massive orca sailed over the protective Plexiglas.

Just like the killer whale, Chet spun his body in midair, cushioning the boy against his chest, making sure his back took the brunt of the fall. He hit the deck with a sharp crack, his breath exploding from his lungs.

Rosario screamed. He couldn't see her but he felt her hand in his own, gripping tightly.

Taka demolished the Plexiglas, beaching herself on the platform.

It felt as if half the water in the tank came with her. Chet, the boy, and Rosario spun away like seaweed caught in an incoming tide.

The pain in Chet's back and chest was excruciating. It felt like getting sandwiched between two cars. His vision wavered as he struggled for air. Cold, fishy water filled his mouth, clogged his ears. Someone tugged on his shoulders, getting him into an upright position.

Eyes stinging from the salty water, he stared in horror as Taka thrashed about, the shattered Plexiglas slicing into her body. Her cries made his soul ache.

She didn't sound distressed or hurt or even angry.

No, Taka sounded…relieved.

Chet looked down at his chest to find the boy clinging to him, his face buried in his soaking wet shirt.

Rosario stood over them, panting, her long black hair dripping water on Chet's face.

"Are you all right?" he said to the boy, worried that he'd crushed him in his attempt to save him.

The boy didn't move or speak.

People were shouting and running, unsure what to do.

Hands trembling, Chet lifted the boy's face from his chest, expecting the worst.

His eyes were closed, mouth set in a thin line.

"Kid. Kid," Chet said, resisting the urge to shake him.

When his eyes fluttered open, Chet felt his own body sag. "Help me up," he said to Rosario, who took his arm and kept him steady. He handed the boy to her.

"Get him back to his parents."

He noticed the boy avoided looking at the suffering orca. Instead, he plastered his face to Rosario's chest.

"What are you going to do?" she asked. Her normally copper skin was pale as death.

His legs were wobbly, the rush of adrenaline making it hard to concentrate. Taka was on her side, her blowhole expelling gas and a spray of crimson mist. An advancing tide of blood was almost at Chet's feet.

Staring at Taka, Chet couldn't find the words to answer Rosario. She said something else to him but he couldn't make out the words.

He watched a once great and majestic creature bleed itself out, her alien language calling out a last farewell to the orcas she'd called family in the holding tank behind them.

CHAPTER TWO

Chet sat naked on his couch, the air conditioner on full blast, watching *True Romance* on his small TV for the hundredth time. He took a long sip of Anchor Steam beer.

"You want some?" Rosario asked, holding the bong out to him. She too was sans clothes, all soft curves and flawless, bronzed skin.

"It's all yours," he said.

She took another long hit, eyes closing and settling deep into the couch, the bong nestled between them.

"I can't go back there," she said.

"Good."

"I mean it. I'd rather wait tables or be a cashier at a gas station than go through that again."

"They would be nobler professions." Chet put a hand on her thigh. She lay her head on his shoulder.

"I'm serious. What happened today, I...I..."

Her eyes shimmered with tears. She'd been crying off and on all day and long into the night. Chet couldn't blame her. This was her first orca suicide. She loved Taka. He was pretty sure Taka loved her back, in the alien way orcas were able to bond with their captors.

Stockholm Syndrome, Chet thought. No, with people like Rosario, it was much more than that. They sensed when someone truly cared for them.

Wrapping his arms around her, Chet kissed the top of her head. It had smelled like fresh berries after they'd come to his apartment and showered, washing the blood and seawater and stench of fear and death from their pores. They hadn't even fooled around in the shower, trading foreplay for an intense scrubbing that left their flesh raw to the touch for an hour after their cleansing of the horror.

"There was nothing you could have done," he assured her.

They'd spent the night consoling one another, anesthetizing themselves with weed and beer and making desperate love. All those crests and crashes should have rendered them unconscious by now, but neither could sleep and they were too sore to fuck.

"You're wrong," Rosario said, wiping her tears away. "I could have quit a long time ago."

"What would that have done?"

"I could have convinced the others to quit, too. If no one was there to care for them, they would have had to close the orca show and set them free."

If only things were that simple. Chet sighed, too tired to vent his frustration at a broken system once again.

"Even if you convinced Chase and Allison and all the others to walk away, there would be a line of people willing to take your place. The only thing that's going to stop it is through legislation. And then again, that will only end it in this country. There are eight other countries that still keep orcas for their amusement."

Rosario bolted from the couch, knocking the bong over. Chet lashed out to grab it before the filthy water spilled all over the cushions.

"But someone has to be the first! If...if we did it, the other countries would follow."

He patted the couch. She plopped down next to him and lay across his bare lap.

Chet said, "Granted, if that ever happened, I'm sure Canada would follow suit. Maybe Norway. But the others? I don't think China and Russia give a shit what we think. If we outlaw it here, though, that's taking care of the lion's share of the issue. We may look to places like China and Russia as the cold hearted bad guys, but in this instance, we're the real monsters."

It was a sad but true fact. Orcas were on display in nine countries, but the United States was home to over half the total of imprisoned killer whales.

"Then that's what I'll do. I'll start a campaign to get a federal law making it illegal to keep orcas and all dolphins in captivity."

He twirled his fingers in her curly black hair. "What will you do for money?"

She kissed his inner thigh. "You'll support me. We'll be a team."

"Oh? I thought you said we needed to keep this casual."

"That was before. Don't tell me you haven't been waiting for me to change my mind."

Chet looked down at the perfect woman draped across his lap. They'd been friends with benefits off and on for the past couple of years. She was right. He'd secretly desired more from their relationship, but didn't dare rock the boat. Rosario was far above his pay grade. She was as smart and funny and caring as she was beautiful. There was no way he was going to say or do anything to ruin what they had.

"So it took a catastrophe to finally get you to realize I'm the love of your life?" he said, wishing he could take it back immediately. She just hinted at them getting more serious and here he was dropping the L word. What an ass. He could always blame the weed later.

She got up and straddled his lap, their noses touching, glassy eyes locked on one another.

"You saved my life. And you did everything you could to save Taka's. You're an incredible man, Mr. Clarke."

They kissed softly, slowly, and Chet realized he wasn't so sore anymore.

CHAPTER THREE

The email was a welcome surprise.

Chet had contracts with all of the marine parks in the western world to give medical consultation on their dolphins and orcas. He was always on call to assist with live births, health crises, deaths, and in Taka's case, mental breakdowns. Orcas in captivity had a slew of health problems that weren't found in the wild. A healthy orca could live up to eighty years.

Not so for the poor creatures stuck in aquariums and marine parks, whose lifespans were cut dramatically due to stress, human interaction and poor living conditions. Man hadn't made a tank large enough to suit the needs of an orca.

It appeared that Sumar, an orca caught in the wild and now trapped at Marine Paradise in Barcelona, was going to give birth to a calf next week. He had been following Sumar's pregnancy all along, but recent events had knocked him sideways. Sure, he'd been witness to orcas acting out to end their lives, but never to such a dramatic and bloody end. Sumar's little miracle had taken a backseat to some big changes.

True to her word, Rosario had quit after returning from the paid week vacation her boss had provided for her nearly being killed. He wasn't surprised by her decision, but he did throw more money at her to change her mind. It didn't work. He'd mistakenly thought that she was leaving her career behind due to some kind of post-traumatic stress. She made it crystal clear that she was tired of being part of the problem, no matter how good her intentions had been.

They'd celebrated her emancipation with a dinner by the ocean at her favorite Italian place, followed by a wild night in her apartment that resulted in a broken shower faucet and cracked box spring.

The Anaheim Dolphinarium was being sued by the sick boy's parents. It had made the rounds on all the local news stations and had even gone national for a night. One of the souvenir shop workers on a break had recorded the whole thing on her phone and given the file to the mother and father. As delighted as Chet would be to see the marine park go under, he knew that if it did, the remaining orcas would just be sold off and shipped to other parks like slaves.

At least Anaheim did a decent job at caring for them. Some of the other options were less than desirable. He cringed at the thought of the Russians getting their hands on them.

He couldn't worry about that now.

First, there was Barcelona.

He wrote back to the president of the park, asking for a second ticket and updated room accommodations in exchange for a reduction in his consulting fee. They were quick to oblige.

Grabbing his cell, he dialed Rosario. She picked up on the first ring.

"What's cookin', good lookin?"

He heard a seagull caw in the distance.

"Where are you?" he asked.

"I went to the beach for a run. Now I'm just catching some rays."

"It's too hot for running."

The heavy breasted weather girl who wore shirts a size too small for her robust frame had said it was going to hit one hundred today. Chet's AC was already having a tough time cutting through the creeping heat.

"You wouldn't run unless someone was chasing you," she said, laughing.

"On a day like today, they could have me."

"It's nice to get all sweaty and just jump in the water."

"Haven't I been making you all sweaty enough?"

"You sure have," she replied, her voice dipping lower, sexier.

"Say, do you have any plans for Friday?"

"Other than signing up for every job board I can find? Nope."

"I may have a job for you. It's temporary, but I think you're well suited to the task."

"I'm almost afraid to ask."

"You ever been to Spain?"

There was a pause. "Nnnnooo."

"Really?"

"I think I'd know if I'd been to Spain. Hell Chet, I've only been out of the country once, and that was to Cabo on spring break."

"Well, get your Spanish to English dictionary, because you're going to Spain."

"For a temp job?" she said, sounding skeptical.

"In a way. I've got a gig assisting with the birth of an orca at a marine park in Barcelona. I told them I needed to bring my experienced assistant."

A gust of wind brought a wave of static over the line.

"Wait, you want me to go back to doing the very thing I just left?"

"In Barcelona."

Her tone worried him. Like an idiot, he thought she'd be blinded by the opportunity to travel to the most beautiful city in Europe.

"In Barcelona," she echoed.

"Look, I know you want what they do to the orcas to end, but this is something special. Just think, you could be there for the birth of the first calf to get its freedom. One of the first humans it looks at may be the person that orchestrates the demise of the worst atrocity ever set upon orcas."

Boy, he really hadn't thought this through. Sweat trickled down his temple.

When she didn't say anything, he repeated, "In Barcelona."

"I can't believe you," she finally said.

All of his enthusiasm vanished like mist under the morning sun.

"Look, I'm sorry for being so dense," he said, trying hard not to stammer over his words. "I should have thought before I spoke. I know how you feel and I shouldn't have thought this would be cool."

"I can't believe you want to take me to Spain," she said with enthusiasm.

"Wait. What?"

His head was spinning.

"Yes!" she cried out.

11

"Yes?"

"Hell yes!"

"But I thought…"

"I was just messing with you. I not only get to go to Spain, but I get to see the birth of a wonderful baby. Oh my God, this is so crazy."

Crazy wasn't the half of it. Chet didn't know whether he was coming or going.

"You almost gave me a heart attack," he said.

Rosario giggled. "That was the idea. Wait, you sure the people there won't be upset that you're bringing your girlfriend?"

Chet felt like a fighter against the ropes. "For one, you're more than qualified to assist me. So no, they don't have any qualms with me bringing a professional to help. And two, are we in boyfriend/girlfriend territory now?"

"Duh. I've slept over your place nine of the past ten nights. I didn't think you needed to give me your school ring to make it official."

Chet sat back in his chair, his grin so wide it hurt. "I'll be damned."

"What? I'm sorry, you cut out for a second there."

"I said come over later so we can put an itinerary together."

She blew a kiss into the phone. "I'll even make dinner. Does shrimp scampi sound good to you?"

"Delicious."

"Good. You might want to hydrate yourself and take a nap before I get there."

She disconnected the call.

Look at that, Chet thought. *And here I thought I was the one giving the big present.*

They landed in Barcelona a couple of days before Chet was scheduled to check in at Marine Paradise. He walked hand in hand with Rosario all through the streets from one end of the city to the other. She spent most of the time with her mouth hanging open, marveling at the incredible beauty of Barcelona.

"Is every building here a work of art?" she asked, as they craned their necks to behold the many spires of Sagrada Familia Church. Construction on the breathtaking masterwork had started in 1882 and was still going on today.

"I always think of Barcelona as Antonin Gaudi's playground," Chet replied, noting some of the changes that had occurred since the last time he had done some sightseeing. "It's kind of crazy to think how one man could alter the landscape of an entire city."

Rosario took an endless stream of pictures on her phone.

"The whole city is a museum," she said. "They should put a dome over it and preserve it."

"If any city should be protected, this is the one."

They stopped at a tapas bar for a late lunch, a cool sea breeze tickling the backs of their necks as they sat outside. The table was filled with small plates of food.

"What's that?" Rosario asked, pointing her fork at a plate of orange cubes sprinkled with herbs.

He speared a cube and popped it in his mouth. "I'm going to say potato. Even if it's not, it's very good."

Their waiter didn't speak English, so Chet had to stumble through ordering with his meager grasp of Spanish. The result was a varied selection of mystery food.

Rosario took a bite, closed her eyes and leaned back in her chair. "It's so good. What's that one by your elbow?"

Staring at the marinated strips of meat, he shrugged. "When it comes to the meat, it's best not to ask. I was taken to my first tapas bar by a colleague at the park years ago. It turned out that my favorite dish, the one I couldn't seem to get enough of, was some animal's balls."

Rosario sputtered laughing, her hand hovering over her mouth to catch any food that might fly out. "You're joking, right?"

"I wish I was."

"You ate balls?"

"Many, many balls over the course of a week."

"And you didn't get sick?"

He took a sip of cold beer. "I admit, I got kind of queasy when I found out what I'd been gorging on for days. Then I realized it didn't matter. It tasted amazing."

"I'm not eating any balls."

Chet waved his hands over the full table. "Odds are, there are some balls here, or at least a tongue or some kind of organ meat. It's best not to ask. Just eat and savor the flavor."

Rosario stared at the food hesitantly, her fork hovering.

"Don't be a wussy," Chet said. "You eat hot dogs. I guarantee you, nothing here is as nasty as what's in a hot dog."

She smiled and jabbed a cube of meat along with some olives. "You're right. I have to stop being so American."

"That's the spirit. And if you really want some balls…"

She rolled her eyes. "You have a one track mind."

"Let it be known, my mind had a whole slew of tracks until you settled in."

"I'll take that as a compliment."

"You should, my little Puerto Rican siren."

They ate tapas and drank beer from icy mugs, walking down to the Plaza de Catalunya to burn off some calories. It was the center of the city, filled with people and park benches. It was famous for the huge number of pigeons that flocked to be fed. Vendors sold bags of breadcrumbs and birdseed. Chet bought a bag and they were soon surrounded by hungry birds. He bought Rosario a single red balloon and a flower he tucked behind her ear. He got a tender kiss that shook him down to his toes in return.

"Let's go walk Las Ramblas," he said.

The long, narrow street was lined with shops and cafés. Mimes dressed in all manner of costumes stood still as statues, tourists trying to get them to flinch.

"It's like a carnival," Rosario said, melting into him.

He pointed to an old building to their right. "I stayed at that hostel once."

"A hostel? Aren't they dangerous?"

"Not all hostels are like those movies. Although, if you don't like strange smells and sleeping with complete strangers, it can be a bit much. But I did find that everyone likes to share their booze at night, so that was a plus."

This was his tenth trip to Barcelona, but it felt like his first. Rosario's wide-eyed enthusiasm infused a feeling of magic within him. It had been a long time since he'd felt anything close to this.

Marine biology had been a foregone conclusion for him at birth. All of the men in his family, going as far back as his great grandfather, had been marine biologists, so naturally, his course was set.

Chet breezed through school because he grew up surrounded by the material. It was part of his DNA. And like his father, he specialized in working with dolphins. Very few people realized that killer whales, or orcas to be precise, were dolphins, not whales. It didn't jive with people to equate smiling, helpful Flipper with a stone cold killer of the sea.

He was good at what he did, but the work was less than exciting, at least to him. Chet knew that people dreamed of traveling the globe and working with dolphins. Meanwhile, he always wondered what it would be like to have the comfort of a cubicle to go to every day where he could just do his job and go home without any heavy moral implications hanging over his head.

Back in his day, Chet's father had been instrumental in assisting with the capture of orcas, filling marine parks with their ill-gotten spoils. That's where Chet and his father parted ways.

Chet wanted nothing more than to set every orca free. He despised what his father did. In direct opposition to his father, he'd consulted with groups in the United States to drum up support for legislation to end their captivity. Now he was introducing Rosario to those groups.

Until there was wholesale change, he knew his skills were best served preserving the health of the orcas that could only dream of being free. They needed someone *on* their side and *by* their side.

And he was sure orcas dreamed. The orcas in his care were brighter than most of the people he knew.

"You want to go back to the hotel?" Rosario said.

"Huh?"

Chet had lost himself in his usual train of troubled thoughts.

"The restaurants won't open for dinner until later and my feet are starting to hurt. I thought we could find something to do that didn't involve walking."

She bent down to drop a coin in a mime's jar. Chet couldn't stop himself from looking down her shirt at her considerable tan cleavage. When she caught him, he turned crimson.

"You dirty little boy," she scolded, slapping his hand.

"Okay, I confess. I have a problem. I need help," he said, wrapping his arm around her waist.

"You see what's under here all the time."

"And I'll never grow tired of it."

That got him another kiss and they headed back in the direction of their hotel.

They just emerged from Las Ramblas when his cell phone started to ring. He rarely got calls. Emails and texts, yes, but very few calls, especially since his mother had passed.

"I better see who this is," he said.

The ID just said it was a private number. He was tempted to swipe the call into voicemail. He wanted to run, not walk, to the hotel.

His thumb hit the answer icon by accident.

"Chet?" a harried voice practically shouted into the phone.

"Yes?"

"This is Ivan Padron, from Marine Paradise. We need you to come right away."

"What's the problem?"

Ivan sounded worried. He breathed heavily into the phone.

"It's Sumar. And the others. Just get here quick!"

The call cut off before Chet could respond. He had a few questions he wanted to ask so he knew what he was walking into.

"Who was it?" Rosario asked.

Chet held up his hand, signaling for a taxi.

"Something's going down with the orcas."

Rosario stopped walking. The balloon string slipped from her fingers. "What does that mean?"

A compact taxi stopped at the curb. "I don't have a clue. But it doesn't sound good."

The red balloon drifted over the city, pushed by the winds as it bobbed over the Mediterranean Sea.

CHAPTER FOUR

Chet and Rosario walked straight into hell.

The stream of cars being herded out of the gates of the marine park told Chet something very bad had happened. Every available hand had been directed to evacuating the park as quickly as possible. Chet spotted a fair number of panicked faces.

Chet's first thought was terrorism. Had someone done something unspeakable to the orcas during the height of the busy season, when the crowds were at their thickest?

They waded against the flow of humanity, pushing their way into the park. No one stopped them. They were more concerned with getting out.

Rosario gasped, stumbling over her own feet as she backpedaled from the madness. Chet alertly grabbed her wrist before she fell.

"What the hell?" she shouted.

The orca tanks were pure, unadulterated chaos.

The water and surrounding decks were awash with blood – all of it, as far as Chet could tell, human.

A trainer, vacant eyes staring directly into the sun, lay at the edge of the tank where they did the orca and dolphin shows. Both of her legs were gone, the stumps trickling blood into the tank.

Another man in his early twenties with curly brown hair tied in a wild bun at the top of his head lurched past Chet and Rosario, the left side of his torso gone. Raw gristle and bone already attracted a horde of flies as the man bumped into Chet. He collapsed with a wet smack, organs spilling from the fatal wound.

Chet stopped a weeping woman from fleeing the scene. Her park uniform was splattered with blood.

"Where's Ivan?" he shouted over the din.

"I...I...let me go!"

She twisted from his grasp, leaping over the fallen half-man and disappearing.

Great spouts of water exploded from the tanks, the water churning as if a massive storm brewed beneath the surface. Orcas breached the surface, slamming onto the deck, giant mouths snapping open and closed, searching for prey.

Chet felt as if he'd been cored out.

"Rosario, you have to get the hell out of here."

She shook her head. "Not without you."

Someone screamed behind them, in the direction of the holding tank where Sumar would be awaiting the birth of her first calf. The scream was cut short, followed by a tremendous splash of water.

He squeezed Rosario's hand. "You don't leave my side, you hear me?"

She nodded, eyes wide with fear.

"This way."

He led them through a Plexiglas gate and into the auditorium, a safe distance from the rampaging orcas. At least he hoped.

Katerina, a ten-year old captive born orca that had always been gentle to the point of timid, shot from the water, smashing her nose into the protective barrier between the auditorium and the tank. Chet's stomach recoiled when he saw her belly had landed on the remains of a park worker, his body exploding like a water balloon. Katerina let loose with a deafening wail before slipping back into the roiling water.

How?

Why?

He spotted her brother, Nootka, swimming round and round, something pale and long locked in his jaws. Chet was pretty sure it was a leg.

Everyone still alive had exited the area. The orcas pounded through the crimson water, mad with blood lust.

"You're too goddamn late," a man shouted.

Chet turned around to see Ivan – pronounced Ee-von (which Chet was lectured about several times) – gripping a rifle.

Ivan Padron had worked at Marine Paradise for most of his adult life, promoted to head man in charge of the orcas and dolphins several years ago. Chet knew Ivan to be a caustic but capable leader who, despite his gruff demeanor, had a real soft spot for the animals in his care. He could be an ass to humans, but when it came to his dolphins, he was a pussycat.

His face was streaked with blood, his long hair plastered to his head. The whites of his eyes peering out from beneath the veil of blood made him look insane.

"What the fuck's happening?" Chet said, wondering if he had to worry about where Ivan was going to point the rifle.

"They've had enough," Ivan replied softly. "And now we've paid the price."

That wasn't any help at all. Yes, orcas had been known to turn on their trainers, killing a handful over the years. But there had never been an outright coordinated revolt. No, that couldn't be the case. Only man was capable of mass slaughter just for the sheer joy of it.

Ivan went to the rail, aimed and shot Katerina before Chet could stop him. He pulled back on the bolt and fired again.

"Wait!" Chet said, reaching for Ivan's arm.

Ivan shoved Chet hard. "Get the fuck off me!"

Rosario tugged Chet to her. "We have to get out of here."

She was right, but he couldn't bring himself to leave. His feet felt as if they'd been cemented to the floor.

Katerina momentarily slid on the deck, scooping the legless woman into her mouth before diving.

Ivan reached into his shirt pocket and extracted two darts. That gave Chet a brief moment of relief. The man didn't want the orcas dead. Despite the carnage they had caused, neither did Chet.

When Nootka leapt straight into the air, Ivan buried a tranquilizer dart in his ivory belly. The orca spun, splashing down on its side before dipping under.

All Chet could do was cling to Rosario while Ivan poured dart after dart into the frenzied orcas. For a while, Chet worried that something had happened to make them impervious to the drugs.

A tense five minutes later, they had settled down. They were still moving, but slowly, no longer interested in eating the many body parts floating in the tank.

"We need to get them out of there before they drown," Chet said.

When orcas slept, one side of their brain would shut down while the other half maintained active breathing. If they didn't compartmentalize sleeping and breathing, they would quickly drown. Remaining active every minute of the day and night was vital for them to survive.

When anesthetized, it was important that they be removed from the water, as the drugs shut their entire brain down.

"We will," Ivan said. "But I'm not going near there to get the retraction unit until I'm positive they're docile."

"What about the pregnant orca?" Rosario said.

Ivan ran a hand down his face. "We'll get to her."

Sumar was in the medical pool that had a rising floor, so Chet knew putting her out and keeping her safe would be a far easier task. Not so in the performance tank.

Ivan stormed off into a tunnel between the rows of seats.

Chet and Rosario watched Katerina and Nootka, their motions getting slower and slower.

"How the hell are three of us going to get them out of the pool?" Rosario wondered, shivering against Chet.

She was right. Removing an orca from a tank required getting them in a sling that was attached to a heavy-duty crane. Depending on the size of the orca, it could take up to a dozen people to perform the delicate maneuver.

"Three of us?" Chet said. "There's no way you're getting in that water."

The water was dyed pink and filled with shredded bits of people. Chet couldn't even imagine himself getting in there. Not without deep psychological scarring that no therapist could ever fix.

The sound of a diesel engine firing up startled them. Ivan must have gotten into the cab of the crane and was bringing it to the tank.

"I want to check the medical pool before he gets here," Chet said.

"It can't be worse than this," Rosario said. "We just have to keep our distance."

Medical pools didn't have all of the safety glass that was supposed to be a barrier between the orcas and their handlers.

They were designed for personnel to have direct access to the orca. The Marine Paradise medical pool didn't have any raised viewing area. If Sumar was affected the same as the other two, and the scream they'd heard earlier was an indication that she was, they would have to be extremely careful.

Chet noticed that Rosario kept her eyes up and in front, careful not to view the human remains at their feet as they slowly made their way to the medical pool.

Lunch at the tapas bar seemed as if it had happened in another lifetime. The food and beer in Chet's stomach had gone sour, turning to acid.

He made sure to keep Rosario behind him when they turned the corner to the medical pool. What he saw robbed the breath from his lungs.

Rosario edged around him, her hand flying to her mouth, instantly sobbing.

It was worse. Far worse.

CHAPTER FIVE

Sumar had given birth to her calf.

At least partially.

The dead orca was half in, half out of its mother. Sumar swam in tight circles, turning the tank into a whirlpool. In the center of the pool were the remains of two people, minus their heads.

"Jesus," Rosario muttered.

Chet's stomach burned at the sight of the flopping calf. He wished to hell Ivan had left him with the rifle so he could settle Sumar down and extract the calf. If things stayed like this for long, there could be significant damage to the mother.

He gripped the railing in front of him and rubbed his eyes.

It was too late to help Sumar or Katerina and Nootka. Once word got out, they would have to be euthanized. It pained Chet to even think about it, no matter what the orcas had done. Because he knew this wasn't them. Something else was happening here. Whether it was some kind of natural or manmade toxin that had affected the orcas at the same time, he couldn't be sure. Whatever it was, it had taken control of their massive bodies and poisoned their minds, gotten them to do things they would never normally do.

It was why Ivan was doing everything he could to tranquilize them. He knew how this would have to end, but he could damn well choose the way it ended. Death by drowning was not a fitting end for the trio of orcas. Better that they put them to sleep painlessly and with some level of dignity.

"No one will understand why," he said aloud.

"Why what?"

He guided Rosario away from the medical pool. There was nothing they could do, nothing more to see.

"We have a long night ahead of us," he said, slumping against a wall.

"How could this happen?"

Rosario's hands quivered as she pushed her hair back.

"I...I don't know. What could drive three healthy orcas utterly mad at the same time? It makes no sense," Chet said.

"They're going to have to be put down, aren't they?"

"Yes, and quickly. Once the police arrive and see what they've done, they'll be ordering us to step aside so they can shoot them."

As if on cue, he heard the approaching bleat of sirens.

He pushed away from the wall, feeling some strength return to his legs. "Come on, let's see what we can do to help Ivan."

The crane was at the edge of the performance tank. Ivan had commandeered seven men from the staff. Only one of them was dressed in an orca trainer's uniform. Chet wondered if she was the only one left alive, or if the others had run for their lives.

A tangle of black wet suits had been thrown on the bloody ground.

Chet came up to Ivan and said, "Where's the rifle?"

"In the cab."

"How many darts you got?"

"Enough for Sumar." Ivan's jaws clenched and unclenched, the hinges popping from the pressure.

"I'll do it," Chet said. "By the time we get Katerina and Nootka out, she'll be ready."

"Make it quick. I need you in the water here."

"I'll be right back," Chet said to Rosario, kissing her forehead. He ran to the cab of the crane, grabbed the rifle and case of tranquilizer darts Ivan had left on the floor.

Ivan barked orders to the nervous men and women as they struggled to get into the wetsuits. Chet was horrified to see Rosario stripping down to her underwear, a wetsuit by her feet.

"You're not going in there," Chet hissed.

When she looked up at him, there was a steely look of determination in her hazel eyes. "The hell I'm not. They need me. Most of these people work the concession stands."

Chet pulled her close so the others couldn't hear.

"There's no way to tell if the orcas are truly out of it. If they wake up while you're in the water, nothing can save you."

She slipped her foot into the wetsuit. "That's where you're wrong. I have you. Now go take care of Sumar so you can get in with me."

There was no time to plead his case against her decision. Plus, she was right. While Ivan operated the crane, the others would need someone who had done this before to guide the orcas into the sling.

"Don't go in until I get back," Chet said.

"Promise."

Chet had to fight the blur of tears as he shot three tranquilizer darts into Sumar. The sight of the lifeless calf broke his heart. He did it quickly, knowing he had to get back to Rosario. When he was done, he let the rifle slip from his fingers. It clattered on the concrete floor.

Just about everyone was in the soup of death that passed for water. Rosario stood at the edge, waiting for him. There was no time to don a wetsuit. He took her hand and they jumped in, careful to keep their mouths tightly closed.

"Fuck, it's cold," Chet said, his muscles seizing for a terrifying moment.

Ivan lowered the massive sling into the water. Chet took control, telling people how to line up around Katerina. He almost gave a loud thanks to God when she didn't awake at their touch. The whole time they worked to guide her into the sling, he kept stealing glances at Nootka. At the first sign of the orca coming to, he was going to shout at everyone to get the hell out of the tank.

Chet, and everyone else, also had to fight the urge to vomit as he waded through strands of viscera. When a half-eaten foot tapped him on the cheek, he had to bite his tongue hard enough to draw blood in order to hold back his scream.

He couldn't help thinking they were in Satan's wading pool, wondering if the demonic beast next to them was going to awaken and devour them.

Katerina was successfully removed. Ivan set her down on the ground and they worked hard to roll her free from the sling. They had all jumped back into the tank to get Nootka when a swarm of police and first responders spilled into the main attraction area of the marine park.

The look of horror and revulsion on their faces would stick with Chet for a long, long time.

"We could use some help here," Chet said. When no one responded, much less moved, the woman next to him repeated his request in Spanish. Two members of the ambulance corps set their stretcher aside, as there would be no need for it, and got into the tank. A police officer followed suit, with the trainer translating for Chet. It was much easier getting Nootka out of the tank.

When they went to the medical pool to get Sumar, everyone stopped. The sight of the calf still partially in its mother's womb took their breath away.

Now that the water was no longer churning, Chet looked for the heads of the two trainers. They were most likely in Sumar's belly.

"We have to do this quickly. She's turning onto her side," Chet said.

Rosario was the first to break the group paralysis, jumping into the bloody pool.

Sumar's blowhole was close to being under water. Once that happened, she would start to drown.

The medical pool had one advantage over the attraction pool – a floor that could be elevated. They wouldn't need the crane to get Sumar out. All they had to do while Ivan started the floor was keep Sumar's blowhole clear.

Mercifully, it didn't take long. Most of the volunteers dropped to their asses and knees, shaking with exhaustion and repulsion.

There was no time for Chet to rest. "Rosario, you think you can help me?"

Her eyes were glassy as she gazed into the distance. She blinked hard and nodded. "I've never done this before."

Chet said, "Not many people have."

Ivan had removed his shirt, the cords of his neck and chest strained from the tension that held him in its grip. A loop of sturdy rope was draped over his shoulder.

"I'll tie this around the calf. The three of us should be able to pull it free."

Chet helped Ivan secure the rope, the infant orca's flesh ice cold to the touch.

Ivan turned to Rosario. "You ever play tug of war?"

"Of course."

"This is the same thing, except losing is not an option."

Chet, Ivan and Rosario dug their heels as best they could on the slippery ground and pulled. At first, the calf didn't move. Ivan grunted, letting out a scream of rage and frustration that almost made Chet drop the rope.

"Come on you son of a bitch!" Ivan wailed.

He wasn't angry at the orca, though Chet was sure that's what everyone that surrounded them supposed. He was mad as hell at whatever pestilence had descended on his beloved orcas, and feeling helpless at the loss of so many precious human lives.

The policeman who had helped them in the tank got a handhold on the rope.

"Pull!" Ivan shouted.

The muscles in Chet's arms burned and quivered. He pulled so hard, spots danced before his eyes.

Something gave way, and suddenly they were on their asses. Chet watched the calf slide out of its mother, riding a tide of gushing fluids. Rosario scrambled to get to her feet and away from the incoming tide.

All Chet could do was lay still, too tired to rise above the swill of afterbirth.

CHAPTER SIX

Marine Paradise had gone from a place of spectacle and wonder to a crime scene that had captured Spain's full attention. News was spreading fast, and within hours of freeing the calf from Sumar, the entire world was aghast with the level of violence that had claimed the lives of the orcas and seven park workers.

Chet and Rosario were questioned by police for the better part of an hour. Someone had brought them cups of coffee as they sat in one of the spectator seats wrapped in fresh towels. Chet didn't think coffee could ever taste this good. The caffeine jolt brought him back from the living dead.

Ivan came storming over to them with a gaggle of police at his heels. They were saying something to him in Spanish but he wasn't paying them any mind.

"What's going on now?" Chet said.

Rosario shrugged. "Sorry, you're dating the one Puerto Rican who can't speak Spanish." She leaned her head onto his shoulder.

"Are you going to assist my marine tech?" Ivan said. His gaze cut like lasers. He should be exhausted, but he looked refreshed and ready to take on the world. Where was he finding the stamina?

"Of course," Chet said.

"She'll be here in a few minutes, if she can get through this madness. Be ready when I call for you."

Chet stared at his empty coffee cup. "Please and thank you."

Ivan's eye twitched and he took off toward Katerina, the police still in tow.

"That was fast," Rosario said.

"Ivan has a Marine Autopsy Technician on staff. I wonder if they'll be able to get through the police barricade."

"I'm sure Ivan will find a way. I'd hate to be the person to tell him no…for anything."

"His bark is worse than his bite." He crushed the cup and dropped it beneath the plastic seat. "Scratch that. His bite is pretty nasty."

"Have you ever done a whale autopsy before?"

"A handful of times. They're not pleasant."

"It can't be any messier than all this," she said, gesturing toward the main tank. Police photographers were taking pictures of bodies and body parts, little yellow flags everywhere. A plastic tarp had been draped over the remains of the trainer who'd had her legs bitten off.

Even though they had stepped under the cold shower beside the medical pool, Chet could still smell the pungent odor of blood and entrails on his skin. It had sunk into his pores. He worried that he'd never be rid of it.

Rosario checked her watch. "I think we're going to miss our dinner reservation."

"We're going to miss a lot of things. I'm sorry it turned out like this."

She laced her fingers between his and kissed his hand. "You have nothing to be sorry for. It's not like you knew this was going to happen. Who in their right mind would? Besides, I got to see you be a hero...again."

"I wouldn't call that being a hero."

"You don't give yourself enough credit. Trust me, most men would have turned tail and run or frozen."

They rubbed noses. It wasn't a romantic gesture, they were too worn out for that. But it felt good to be close, to be touching. Chet said, "You're not so bad yourself, diving right into that tank."

"I'm going to spend the rest of my life trying to forget that."

The heat of the afternoon sun had given way to a dull orange glow and cooling sea breeze. They heard Ivan shout above the din, "We need lights!"

While they waited for the marine tech, Chet and Rosario watched the police wheel in an array of metal halide light carts. They were set up around the two tanks. Chet knew that when it got dark, the moment those lights were turned on, it would be brighter than the noonday sun.

His body was starting to stiffen up from sitting around. He got to his feet and stretched, his muscles feeling as if he'd spent ten hours in a gym. His neck, back and knees cracked.

"We're going to need a couples' massage before we head back home," Rosario said, taking his cue and shaking the weariness from her limbs.

"Make that a couple of couples' massages."

Ivan had found his shirt and tied his hair back with a rubber band. He stepped to the wall separating the seats from the main stage and crooked a finger at Chet.

"Duty calls," Chet said. "Look, why don't you go back to the hotel and try to get some sleep? This is going to take a while."

"I'll rest when you rest. Until then, you're going to show me how this whole autopsy thing works."

They made their way toward Ivan. "I don't suppose there's any way I can talk you out of this?" Chet said to her.

"Nope."

"I didn't think so."

They stepped over the low barricade, Ivan lending a hand to help Rosario, proving he had a bit of a gentleman lurking within.

"My tech is already with Sumar," Ivan said. "I'll take you to her."

They had to tread carefully through the police and crime scene markers.

Chet said, "Ivan, how did all of this start?"

"I wasn't here to see it, but from what I can tell, the orcas went crazy all at once, right when the second show of the day began. One second they were leaping for the rings suspended above the tank, the next, they turned on my people. Someone said it looked like the attack had been planned."

"Planned? They hunt in coordinated packs in the wild, but I can't see them plotting out a...a revolt like this ahead of time, then knowing exactly when and how to strike. Sumar was in the medical pool. When did she start up?"

"The same exact moment."

Ivan's tone implied he didn't want to talk about it further. When they arrived at the medical pool, an attractive blonde woman was kneeling by the calf. Several black bags were secured to a handcart.

"This is Raquel Suarez. Raquel, this is Chet Clarke, the marine biologist from the States. And...and..."

"Rosario Benitez, Chet's assistant," Rosario said, extending a hand.

Raquel was young, under thirty, with sharp features and ice blue eyes that shone from behind a pair of pink-framed eyeglasses. She shook Rosario's hand, then Chet's. Her grip was firm to the point of painful.

"I believe we met once before," Raquel said to Chet. "Was it at that conference in Norway?"

That had been three years ago and Chet had been a paid speaker. He'd met so many people his brain went on name and face overload.

"Oh yes, I thought you looked familiar," Chet said.

The marine tech flashed a quick smile and pushed her glasses against the bridge of her nose. "I guess we'll get started," Raquel said with just a slight Spanish accent. She went about opening the cases containing the necessary tools.

Rosario whispered, "You have no idea who she is."

"Is it that obvious?"

"Painfully."

Ivan shouted at someone to turn on the lights beside the medical pool. Chet had to shield his eyes when they snapped on.

"We'll start with the calf," Raquel stated matter-of-factly, holding a scalpel the size of Chet's forearm.

"You sure you want to watch this?" Chet asked Rosario.

"No. But I'm staying just the same."

They watched Raquel cut deep into the calf's torso. After being surrounded by so much carnage, the smell didn't even make Chet flinch.

Grabbing a deep plastic tub, he set about helping Raquel collect the organs.

CHAPTER SEVEN

Sitting down to sift through his email account was always heavy lifting for Jamel Abrams. Aside from the dozens, if not a hundred or more, direct emails that came to him on a daily basis were the score of automatic alerts he had set to keep him apprised of the secret world that existed right under everybody's noses.

The alerts were divided into numerous categories. Each would send him links to stories that concerned: strange weather, animal die-offs, chemtrails, psychic phenomena, major storm warnings, earthquakes and many, many more esoteric happenings. He was good at skimming the topline of a story and separating the wheat from the chaff, but it still took time.

The Internet was great for gathering information. It was also bogged down with a nightmarish load of chaff. It had taken Jamel some time to program certain websites to be ignored. In the world of conspiracy theories, the thin line between informed and paranoid seemed as fine as silk. The general public may have derided conspiracy theorists as the 'tin foil hat people', but in Jamel's community, they knew who really had the shiny heads.

Not that Jamel considered himself a conspiracy theorist.

What he knew to be true was a stone cold fact. No theories needed.

The truth was *in* there. He just needed to find a way to get it *out*.

His grunt job at a filling station left him plenty of time, and brain power, to do the real, necessary work. It was why he'd become the master of odd jobs, a far cry from the life his parents had mapped out for him. If they only knew. Sometimes, he wished to hell he could clue them in to the truth, but plausible deniability was essential.

His computer chimed that a Skype call was coming in. He opened the application and saw it was his east coast cohort, Sam, who went by the Skype handle IN2MNDCTRL. Jamel accepted the video call request and a window popped up displaying Sam sitting by her dining room bay window. Her yard was a virtual forest. A cardinal pecked away at food in her bird feeder.

"You just get home?" Sam asked, sipping from a glass of iced tea. She was a retired schoolteacher with the beatific face of your favorite aunt or grandma. Only in this modern age of technology, information sharing and remote communication could she and Jamel have become friends.

"Literally walked in the door. Looks hot by you."

Sam looked over her shoulder and the bird flew away. "Summer came early. It's a perfect day for sun tea."

He held up a paper bag, its soggy bottom stained with grease, and a cup of coffee. "I've got the breakfast of champions here. I'd make sun tea if I could find the sun."

Anchorage, Alaska was not the place to be if you enjoyed warm summer days. Jamel had been here so long, he'd forgotten what it was like to break out in a sweat.

"Well, I have something that I think will brighten your day." She tapped on her keyboard and an email instantly popped up in Jamel's inbox. "I know it's early for you, so people probably haven't heard about this one yet."

Jamel opened the email and saw five links. Nothing was labeled but he could tell from the URLs that they were from reputable websites.

"What do we have here?"

"That's exactly what I said," Sam said.

Jamel scanned the first article, the headline reading: KILLER WHALES LIVE UP TO THEIR NAME!

He felt his heartbeat quicken. The article went on in graphic detail about a trio of killer whales that had turned on their trainers in the middle of a show at a marine park in Barcelona. Seven people were dead, many more injured. The whales were immediately euthanized and autopsies were being conducted. There was no explanation for the revolt of the killer whales and it was too early to even speculate.

Sam sat quietly while Jamel read each article. The others were pretty much a rehash of the first, though one of them did have a grainy picture of several people gathered around a whale that lay on its side on the ground. There appeared to be a long gash in its belly.

When he finished, he popped the lid off his coffee and took a long drink.

"What a nightmare."

Sam cringed. "I can't even imagine. Just think, the park was filled with little kids. They watched those trainers get eaten alive. The poor dears."

"Three killer whales, all going postal at the same time." Jamel tugged at the coarse hairs on his chin. "That seems kinda odd, don't you think?"

"Look at paragraph five in the CNN article."

He clicked into the tab with the CNN link. When he read paragraph five, his right eyebrow lifted as high as it could go.

"You're shitting me?"

"Language," Sam scolded with a light smile.

"The third whale was in another tank. How is it possible that they all decided to attack at the same time? Can whales plan and remember something like that?"

"Actually, killer whales aren't whales at all," Sam said, ever the teacher. "In fact, they're members of the dolphin family. I've always found it odd that we call them killer whales, when in reality they're *whale killers*. They're apex predators that will attack anything in the sea. There have been instances where captive killer whales have attacked trainers, but only one attack on one person. Never has there been a case of mass murder by multiple killer whales."

Mass murder.

The thought of it made Jamel shiver.

Jamel's fingers were itching to hit the keyboard and start doing research. He'd have to wait until he disconnected the call with Sam.

"Are you sure of that?" he asked.

"Positive. I did some digging while you were sleeping. It's unprecedented."

"In captivity, but how about in the wild?"

Sam bent closer to her keyboard, keys clacking. Another email landed in Jamel's inbox.

"Just a few links on orca behavior. They're known to hunt in packs, or more correctly, pods. They'll zero in on a walrus or shark or even a whale three times their size and work in tandem to take it down. One of the videos I sent you was taken by a drone as it hovered over a pod attacking a beluga whale. The pod contained fourteen killer whales. They divided into two groups. One group would surround the beluga, keeping it surrounded. They'd repeatedly smash into it, trying to induce internal bleeding. In between body blows, they would leap on top of the whale, dunking it under water so it couldn't breathe."

Jamel opened the video file and was transfixed.

"They were trying to drown it?"

"Exactly," Sam said. "And while the first group attacked, the other would stay to the side to catch their breath and recharge. When they were ready, they'd relieve the first group to continue the assault."

He couldn't believe what he was seeing. The only time he'd seen killer whales was in the movies. *Free Willy* and *Orca* were the extent of his knowledge, and he knew that *Orca* was just a cheesy B-movie that had no basis in reality.

What he was watching was a highly intelligent assault, deftly organized by the pod of whales.

No...dolphins.

The scene was as brutal as it was awe-inspiring. The water churned around the trapped beluga. Killer whales both big and small took turns battering it with their heads and massive tail fins. He could see the whale desperately trying to expel gasses and take in air from its blowhole as it was repeatedly shoved under the surface.

"I can't believe this," he said.

"They call them the wolves of the sea for a reason. If you fast forward to the end, you can see that the whole pod shares in the victory. It took them over an hour to kill the whale, but once they did, every member got their share."

He moved the scroll bar to just a few minutes shy of the end and stared in rapt fascination as each killer whale took its turn feasting off the beluga carcass. As brutal as it looked, he realized that like man, killer whales had to eat. And like man, they were the apex predators of their domain. There was nothing against nature with feeding your family.

Even though it was shot from a distance, he was shocked by how much blood was in the water.

He ended the video and settled into his chair. The breakfast sandwich he'd gotten at Nancy's Diner had lost its appeal.

"They can do all that to a whale, but they've never tried to attack a person in the water like that?"

Sam shook her head. "Not that I could find."

If Sam couldn't find it, it didn't exist. She was a master at research.

"Why do you think they don't attack boats like that?" he asked.

"I guess boats don't look as yummy. Their DNA isn't programmed to hunt artificial objects. Even when they're on the hunt, people can be in kayaks close to them and not be touched. It's really pretty incredible."

"Which makes what just happened in Spain all the more remarkable."

"Exactly. I don't know if it has any correlation to what we're looking for, but it's worth keeping an eye on."

Jamel's computer screen was filled with open windows related to killer whales and the Barcelona story.

They've been manipulated somehow, he thought. *No disease or brain disorder can make three animals flip a switch to psycho killer at the same time. No fucking way. This was done on purpose. I can't wait to see what bullshit excuse they eventually give to explain this away.*

The killer whale story had moved to the top of his 'to-watch' list. He thanked Sam and promised to keep on top of the story as it progressed.

All of his other emails could wait.

This bore some special attention.

CHAPTER EIGHT

Chet and Rosario didn't get back to their hotel until five in the morning. Ivan had driven them across town, the car shrouded in silence. They were too exhausted to speak.

Rosario set the alarm on her phone for noon. When it went off, singing *Sweet Child O' Mine*, Chet's first instinct was to chuck it across the room. It felt as if he'd just gotten under the sheets.

"Wakey, wakey," Rosario said. Her eyes were still closed and it looked as if she hadn't moved a muscle since hitting the bed.

"That's easy for you to say."

Chet lifted his head off the pillow and his body came alive with a cascade of aches and pains that went all the way down to the arches of his feet.

When he tried to stretch his arms, he had to quickly pull them back to his sides. It felt that if he stretched too far, something would snap.

"I don't think I can get up," he said, half-joking.

Groaning as she rolled onto her side, Rosario managed to get to her feet.

"I think I'm broken," she said, her hair a wild mess, face hidden, arms hanging limply like a sleepwalker.

"Come back to bed," Chet grunted when he leaned over to take her hand, pulling her back onto the rumpled sheets. "I'll get us some water and ibuprofen. We're going to have to take this in stages."

She lay next to him, her warm hand in his, blowing a curl from her eyes.

"Ivan said he'd be here at one."

Chet got up and stumbled to the mini fridge, getting two cold bottles of water. He grabbed some pills from his toiletry kit in the bathroom. "An hour is plenty of time for these to work and feel somewhat human again."

While they drank and willed the aches and pains to go away, they talked about the autopsy. Doing an autopsy on four whales was no easy feat. Chet had done all he could. The rest was up to Raquel and the tense wait for lab results.

He was amazed at how Rosario hadn't shied away not just from the autopsy, but all of the madness that had erupted at Marine Paradise. She was a remarkable woman, and he was grateful she was with him. He wasn't sure how he would have handled all of this alone.

"I think any answers we find are going to come from the brain analysis," Chet said, wincing when Rosario laid her head on his bare chest. "Unless they were drugged, in which case toxicology will come up with a culprit."

"Even if they were doped with something, no drug could coordinate the exact time when they would lash out."

"Which is exactly why I'm putting my money on the brain."

She finished her water and took his empty bottle. "What do you think they'll find?"

"Something we've never seen before."

They had just enough time to shower, get dressed and gobble down room service of sliced ham, olives and bread before meeting Ivan in the lobby. He wore a loose fitting cotton shirt and tan slacks. Unlike them, he didn't look like he'd gone ten rounds with Mike Tyson.

"I think the park has more cops than it did yesterday," he said, pushing his hair back. "It's a goddamn nightmare." Even though Ivan had been born and raised in Spain, he'd spent a considerable amount of time in New York and Florida during his twenties and early thirties. He definitely had the colorful vernacular of a New Yorker, all without the trace of an accent.

They climbed into his compact car, gripping the seats as he whizzed through the streets of Barcelona. A majority of the vehicles on the road were brightly colored Vespa scooters. Chet held his breath as they nearly clipped a score of Vespas and their unfortunate riders.

He didn't dare tell Ivan to slow down. Knowing him, that would only encourage him to speed up.

Ivan informed them that Marine Paradise would be closed indefinitely. The entrance was blocked by two police cars. News vans were everywhere. After a few words with the police Chet couldn't understand, they let Ivan drive through the barricade.

"Fucking vultures," Ivan said, staring down the throng of reporters with microphones held out toward his car. "What more do they want? They already have their pound of flesh…literally."

It was an exceptionally hot day. Chet had taken a shower twenty minutes ago and already felt like he needed another.

As they walked into the park's main offices, Chet asked, "I meant to ask you last night, how are Punch and Judy?"

"Gone," Ivan said, walking so fast, they could barely keep pace with him.

"Who are Punch and Judy?" Rosario asked.

"Bottlenose dolphins. They've been here for years. You'd love them. Or would have."

"What happened to them?" Rosario asked.

Ivan stopped, turning on his heels. "I had to sell them to a marine park in Chile last year. We had a bad season. It was either them or let some staff go. I've been running things as lean as possible as it is. Any less staff and the animals wouldn't get the proper care." His eyes glazed over and he stared at the wall over Rosario's shoulder.

No doubt thinking about the seven people he lost yesterday, Chet thought. *And the lawsuits that will inevitably follow. Marine Paradise is never going to reopen. After all of the unpleasantness that Ivan will have to go through in the following weeks, the light at the end of his tunnel is unemployment.*

He turned to Chet and curtly said, "Why do you ask?"

"Because they're dolphins. I was wondering if they were affected in any way at the same time as the orcas."

Ivan patted him on the shoulder. "Yes, you're right. If they were here, that would have been my first question as well. Forgive me. Come, let's see if Raquel has anything for us."

Chet reached for Rosario's hand as they walked the corridors back to where the marine veterinary suites were located. Raquel Suarez was alone, hunched over a microscope.

"Well?" Ivan said irritably.

Raquel looked up, adjusting her glasses.

"So far, nothing."

"How is that possible?"

"Everything I've observed, from organs to tissue, looks normal. They were healthy animals."

Chet looked around at the staggering number of sealed plastic tubs they'd filled the night before. Sections of organs floated in preservative fluids. He wondered if Raquel had even gone home. She was wearing a stained lab coat, so he couldn't tell if she had on the same clothes as yesterday.

"What about their brains?" Chet asked. Rosario walked over toward an examination table where a hunk of Katerina's hide now sat. From the look of things, Raquel had been working on it before they'd intruded.

"Visually, I can't find anything abnormal. I did have a chance to thoroughly review Nootka's. No parasites, no growths."

Ivan kicked a rolling cart and sent it spinning, making everyone jump.

"We all saw there was *something* fucking wrong with them! I'm going to have to answer to the families of seven people...seven good people. *Mierda*! Make that the entire country. Everyone wants answers."

"You can't blame Raquel," Chet said. "Do you want her to just make something up?"

There was a tense moment when it looked as if Ivan were about to pick up a tray filled with dissection tools and throw it against the wall. No one spoke or moved.

He glared at Chet, then his shoulders softened.

"You're right. You're right," Ivan said, dropping the tray.

Chet heard Rosario let out a loud exhale.

"Something will turn up," Chet said. "Until then, I'll assist Raquel as best I can. I know everyone is screaming for the why of it all, but this may take time."

Ivan checked his watch and spluttered a string of curses in Spanish. "I have to be at a press conference in ten minutes. Then I'm going to visit each of the families. If I survive today..."

He stormed out of the suite.

"I feel bad for him," Raquel said.

"Me, too," Chet said. He pulled some gloves from a box and handed a pair to Rosario. "So, let's do whatever we can to help him."

CHAPTER NINE

The skies had darkened and their bellies were grumbling when Chet, Rosario and Raquel came to the conclusion they had done all they could, at least for today. Five visiting marine veterinarians had stopped in at different times to offer their assistance. This was Raquel's court, and Chet at first worried how she would react.

It turned out he'd watched too many movies where the local cops bristled when the feds swooped in to take over. Raquel was of the belief that the more informed minds dedicated to solving this puzzle, the better. So many theories had been bandied about, Chet was at a loss to remember even a third of them.

The last of the vets, a retired gentleman with wild, Einstein hair white as cotton, had left an hour ago, shaking his head and muttering in Spanish. He spoke no English, but Chet saw plain as day that the man was frustrated.

Luckily, Rosario had been writing down what she could understand all along on a legal pad that was now crammed with notes.

"I'll go through them, type them out so they make sense and send you the file," she said to Raquel as they tossed their filthy lab coats in the laundry bin.

Raquel gave an appreciative sigh. "*Salud.*"

"I know that one," Rosario said. "It means 'bless you', right?"

"Very good."

"I used to love to watch *Sabado Gigante* as a kid," Rosario said. "I had no idea what was going on but it was manic and colorful. I picked up a few words."

"I used to watch it, too," Raquel said with a tired grin. It was the first smile she'd cracked all day...not that there had been anything to smile about. "I liked the dancing most. Ivan drove you here, didn't he?"

"He did," Chet said, his hand on Rosario's shoulder, feeling the hard ball of tension there.

"I'll drive you to your hotel. Or wherever you want to go."

Chet's stomach made a gurgling protest. "As you can hear, I need to feed Seymour."

Neither woman got his reference to *Little Shop of Horrors*.

"Before your time," he said. *Before* my *time*, he thought. "How about I treat us all to dinner? Raquel, you're the local. Where do you suggest we go?"

Normally, inviting a beautiful woman out to dinner with your new girlfriend would be considered a major faux pas. Nothing about this situation was normal.

"If it's all right, I'd rather just go home, eat some soup, have a smoke and go to bed," Raquel said. "I don't think I'd be very good company."

Have a smoke. Chet knew what that meant. He could use one himself. Just touching Rosario's shoulder told him she could, too. What was the etiquette when it came to asking someone you knew less than a day and after autopsying orcas to share their stash?

His head hurt just contemplating it. Best to just pretend he hadn't heard it.

"I understand. I have a feeling we won't be world class conversationalists either," he said instead.

"Where are you staying?"

"The Catalonia Square," Rosario said.

"I'm going to assume you're not in the mood for seafood."

They walked out the door, breathing in fresh air for the first time in almost ten hours. It was still warm, but the moon glow softened the heat's edge.

"That would be a good assumption," Chet said.

"I know a pretty good steakhouse by your hotel. It's only a block away. I can take you there."

"Thank you, that sounds perfect," Rosario said.

The vast parking lot was empty save Raquel's car. Chet pulled up short when he looked over toward the entrance.

"Looks like we'll still have to run through the gauntlet."

The entrance was lit bright as a baseball diamond during a night game. The news crews looked to have doubled since the afternoon. He wondered if the locals were now joined by international syndicates.

Raquel spat a string of what he could only assume were curses under her breath.

"I can only imagine the rumors they're spreading," she said, opening the car doors with a click of a button on her key fob.

"Which is why Ivan is going to be a hard ass until we get him some hard proof of what made them turn," Chet said, settling into the back seat. Rosario took the front, reaching back to take his hand.

"I can't imagine how he's feeling right now," Rosario said. She was right. No matter how bad they thought their day had been, it was nothing compared to what he had to go through. Visiting the families of his staff that had been killed must have worn him down to a dull nub.

Raquel angled the car so it was directly facing the barricade.

"Maybe I should just drive straight through them," she said. Her tone was flat, her face serious.

"That should get them to scatter," Chet joked.

The joke was on him when Raquel gunned the engine, tires screeching, the stench of scorching rubber billowing through the open windows.

Chet fumbled in the back seat, looking for his seat belt.

"Maybe you should slow down," he said.

Rosario planted a hand on the dashboard. "Raquel, what are you doing?"

The marine tech sneered. "I haven't slept in over forty-eight hours and I've seen things I can never forget. I think I've earned the right to blow off a little steam."

"By running people over?" Chet exclaimed.

She had flicked on the brights, the twin beams captivating the tight gaggle of reporters and police. Many of them shielded their faces from the sharp glare.

Chet's heart slammed against his chest. He considered reaching over and taking control of the wheel, but that wouldn't do squat to slow them down. Plus, he'd probably end up flipping the car over, taking out more people than if they just hit them head on.

Rosario somehow remained calm, though there was a sharp edge to her voice. "Okay, joke's over Raquel. Either turn away or slow the hell down."

Raquel didn't reply, but Chet's mouth went dry when he saw the needle on her speedometer jump up a few more kilometers per hour.

"Cut the shit," he wailed, his voice cracking as if he were back in puberty. He grabbed ahold of Rosario's shoulders as if he could prevent her from flying through the windshield on impact any better than her seatbelt.

Some reporters had started to scatter, but they were thwarted by the crush of people and equipment. Chet thought he saw one of the cops go for his gun.

Holy shit!

Sleep deprivation or some kind of post-traumatic stress had caused Raquel to snap. And now, even if they somehow didn't mow down a slew of people, they were going to be shot. Chet wished to hell he had taken the front seat and Rosario was in the safer position in the back.

Rosario barked, "Slow…the fuck…down…now!"

The cop now had his gun out, pointing at the car. Cameras and lights had swiveled, the barreling car now the focus of the news.

Chet wanted to turn away, but couldn't. "Holy Christ!"

Just as they were about to hit terminal velocity, Raquel downshifted, cutting the wheel hard and veering to the left of the captive targets. The rear of the car fishtailed. Chet knew she was going to lose control and they were going to slam into the barricade and people on his and Rosario's exposed side of the car.

In the scant flash it took to pass by the stunned crowd, time seemed to stand still.

He saw the policeman's hand tremble as he realized he didn't need to shoot the encroaching vehicle.

A female reporter dropped her microphone, burying her face in her cameraman's chest, awaiting the inevitable.

There were some screaming faces, but most were wide-eyed and mute, powerless to save themselves, resigned to their fate.

And just like that, they disappeared in a cloud of burning tires and asphalt.

The car zoomed along the perimeter of the parking lot's fence.

Raquel let out a low giggle.

Chet wasn't sure he could breathe. It felt like something was jammed in his throat. Rosario still had her fingers dug into the hard plastic of the dashboard.

"What the hell was that?" she shouted.

"Maybe now they'll go away," Raquel said.

Chet had to practically pry his tongue from the roof of his mouth. "Or, maybe they'll call in reinforcements to cover the story of the crazed lunatic who tried to go all *Death Race 2000* on them!" He twisted around to look out the narrow back window. All he could see were the lights from all the news crews. "Now how do we get out of here without getting arrested?"

"No worries," Raquel said. "I know another way."

She swerved to avoid a row of speed bumps. Chet and Rosario bounced around the car.

True to her word, there was a small exit to the rear of the aquarium that must have been used for deliveries. No one was covering that side of the marine park. They sailed through the slim gate, the car jouncing as it ate up the pavement.

She slowed down to a normal speed, cruising down the mostly empty streets to the center of Barcelona.

"My father raced cars for a living," she finally said as way of explanation. "He taught me everything. I had dreams of following in his footsteps, but he begged me not to do it."

"I'm sure he didn't teach you to scare the shit out of innocent people who thought you were going to kill them," Rosario said. Like Chet, she sounded more relieved than angry. A brush with death could do that to you.

"I'm what you call...how do you say it in America...an adrenaline junkie."

"No," Chet said, "We call that lunacy."

Raquel laughed. "Don't worry. No one was hurt, were they?"

As shaky as he was, he had to admit, the only things that had been harmed were the tires.

Raquel dropped them off in front of the steakhouse without so much as an apology. She uttered an innocent goodnight before driving away.

Rosario looked to Chet, slowly shaking her head. "That bitch is crazy."

He hugged her, feeling the tension slowly melt away and she wrapped her arms around him.

They staggered into the packed steakhouse and were lucky to get a table. Chet had been to Spain numerous times and still couldn't believe how late the natives had their dinner. Back home, restaurants would be thinning out by now, not humming in the shank of the evening.

A glass of wine helped take some of the edge off, but not enough to quell Chet's private worries.

He didn't know Raquel, so there was no way to tell if what had just happened was par for the course.

If it wasn't, then what came to him next was far more frightening than almost killing a crowd of reporters and police.

What if whatever had affected the whales had somehow infected them?

How long would it be before he and Rosario turned on the people around them, or each other?

CHAPTER TEN

By the time the steak arrived, along with a side of crispy potatoes and vegetable medley tossed in olive oil, Chet's appetite had vanished. Yes, his body was a bit on the trembly side, his stores of energy as empty as No Man's Land. But creeping dread had kicked his hunger aside, and nothing could make him swallow more than a few mouthfuls.

"Are you feeling alright?" Rosario asked, tucking into her filet.

"I think I'm more tired than hungry," he lied.

"I'll be able to sleep for days after this meal. Come on, you sure you don't want to try a little of mine?"

He waved off the fork of meat she hovered over his plate.

"I'm sure."

While Rosario ate, he kept worrying that his loss of appetite was the first sign of infection. It was ludicrous and completely self-inflicted paranoia, but he couldn't stop himself. The runaway train to Anxiety Station had ditched the brakes and was heading down the tracks at death defying speed.

When the waiter asked if they wanted dessert, Rosario took one look at him and declined. He could see she was disappointed but didn't want to keep him in the restaurant any longer than she had to.

"You look pale," she said as she got up to go to the ladies' room.

"I do?" He had to control himself not to sound like a frightened fool. What he couldn't stop was the line of sweat beads from breaking out on his forehead.

"Yes, you do," she said, her brows creased with worry. "You need some rest. I think you've hit the wall."

Looking at his full plate, he sipped from his water glass, hoping to hide the fear in his eyes.

"I'll be quick. Then it's to bed for you. And not the fun kind of *to bed*." She kissed his forehead. "Well, at least you don't have a fever."

The moment she stepped away, he used his napkin to soak up the perspiration on his face and the back of his neck.

I don't have a fever. That's a good thing, right?

For the life of him, he couldn't figure out where this was coming from. He'd never been known to be a hypochondriac. Then again, he'd never seen anything like what happened back at Marine Paradise.

He noticed his hand trembling as he laid his napkin back across his lap.

"Get your shit together, man," he hissed.

"Pardon?"

Of course their waiter had chosen that exact moment to cozy up to the table.

"No-nothing. Just the check, *por favor*."

Rosario came back and he paid with cash so he didn't have to wait for his card to be run through the machine. They walked back to the hotel. It was a beautiful night, a hint of the salty Mediterranean on the silky breeze. Rosario talked while he listened, hoping his legs didn't give out, fearing that his mental and physical breakdown were sure signs that he was about to turn into a homicidal maniac.

Would there be enough warning to get the hell away from Rosario before he hurt her?

Was all this the very warning that he was choosing to ignore? He took her offered hand as they entered the hotel lobby, hoping he wouldn't turn on a dime and rip it out of its socket in a fit of uncontrollable rage.

Would the mania that had ultimately led to the demise of the three orcas hit him like a hammer blow from behind? Would he in turn bash Rosario like a hammer blow from behind?

His swirling thoughts only added to his nausea, turning his muscles to expired yogurt.

Somehow, he managed to open their door, heading straight for the bed and plopping on his back.

"I'm starting to worry about you," Rosario said as she stood over him. His eyes were closed, his breathing ragged. "I'll get these clothes off and tuck you in."

He was doing what he could to help her get his shirt off when his cell phone started chirping. It was after midnight. Hardly a time for social calls.

Assuming it would be one of his friends back home where it was nine hours earlier, he ignored it. Rosario had hustled into the bathroom to get him a glass of water and some aspirin. He'd started out a mess and he was ending the day in even worse shape.

Do I tell her? he thought. *She has a right to know. If it's happening to me, it can happen to her.*

When she came back into the room, his phone went off again.

"Someone wants to talk to you," she said, plucking the phone from his hand. Her eyebrow rose when she looked at the display. "It's Ivan."

That didn't allay his fears. His stomach, already turned over twice, dropped to his knees.

He took the phone from her and swiped the screen to answer. Before he could say hello, Ivan was blurting, "Turn on the television!"

The less than tactful order snapped him from his delirium.

"What?" Chet said.

"Go to Telecinco. Quick."

"Rosario, can you hand me the remote?"

"Sure. What's going on?" She grabbed the remote from the top of the TV and tossed it to him. He caught it with a remarkably steady hand.

"I don't know, but I don't think Ivan is calling to recommend a good movie to watch."

"I wish to Christ I was," Ivan said. "Are you watching?"

"Hold on." Chet fat fingered the control but eventually found the station. There was breaking news coverage with a live feed from what appeared to be an offshore oil rig. "What the hell am I looking at, Ivan?"

He couldn't figure out how to get the closed captioning for English. The video, taken from a helicopter high above the rig, showed a brightly lit platform above a pitch black sea.

"That's a new oil rig at Algarve, just off Portugal's southern coast. Hold on, they'll get a good shot in a second."

Chet had put Ivan on speaker. Rosario said, "A good shot of what?"

True to his word, the camera shifted, zooming in on one of the sturdy legs of the rig. Now they could see the water boiling, white caps exploding everywhere. Someone had directed a spotlight on the water.

The hump of an orca flashed briefly into the light. Rosario gasped as it smashed the rig with the top of his head and disappeared.

It wasn't alone.

Chet couldn't be sure because of the unsteady camerawork and bad lighting, but it looked like there had to be at least a half dozen orcas down there.

"They're attacking an oil rig?" he said, no longer thinking about his impending spiral into madness and death.

"It started three hours ago," Ivan said. "There was a pod of eight at first. Then it was joined by another pod of eleven. You can't see them now because they're on the other side of the rig, maybe resting. About fifteen minutes ago, a third pod came into the picture. They're estimating there are a dozen or more in this new pod."

The orcas took turns assaulting the unyielding rig, oblivious to the pain.

Multiple orca pods congregating wasn't that uncommon.

Dozens of orcas trying to batter a manmade structure in the middle of the sea was.

"Are there any more coming?" Rosario asked, sitting on the edge of the bed and gripping both her knees until her knuckles went white.

"That's the problem," Ivan's tinny voice replied. "They think there may be as many as a hundred or more heading their way."

"What?" Chet said, pacing the room. "Did you say a hundred or more?"

"Best estimates we can get in the dark."

Chet had heard of multiple pods temporarily getting together that numbered up to two-hundred. This, however, seemed like a suicide mission. They couldn't possibly knock down the rig.

Could they?

"Are you dressed?" Ivan said.

Chet's eyes felt as if they had been peppered with sand. He didn't know if it was from exhaustion or his forgetting to blink while he watched the spectacle on the television.

"Yeah," he said. "We actually just got in."

"Good. Meet me in the lobby."

"Why?"

"Because we're going to the oil rig. Whether we get there in time to witness the orcas or are there for the aftermath is up to the orcas."

An extreme close-up showed an orca hitting the rig so hard, there was a visible crack in its skull.

Rosario sniffled. Chet saw the tears on her face.

"Wait, you said we're going to the rig?"

"I got a call from the head of the oil company. Since we faced something similar, he's paying for us to go there and figure out what the hell is going on."

Chet was lightheaded. He hoped it was simply because he'd prevented himself from eating.

"When will you get here?" he said, too numb to fully take in everything that was happening around him.

"I just pulled up to the hotel. Hurry up. Our plane leaves within the hour."

CHAPTER ELEVEN

A private jet awaited them at Barcelona Airport, courtesy of the CEO of AOI, also known as American Oil Industries. Chet and Rosario followed Ivan onto the sleek jet in a daze.

Were they really heading to Portugal in the dead of night to witness a mass orca suicide?

They continued to watch the live news coverage on the flight over the gold plated laptop provided by the flight attendant. There was no official representative of AOI on the flight, though they were told someone would be there to meet them in the morning.

The short flight ended in Faro Airport, where they were then whisked into a waiting helicopter by a harried looking man in a suit who said he worked for AOI.

"Aren't you coming with us?" Chet asked as the doors were being shut.

The man just shook his head as he walked away, the wash from the spinning blades making his hair look like Medusa's snakes.

"He was a real pleasant fucking chap," Ivan said. "You'd think with all these extravagant toys, they could afford to give us some top shelf liquor."

Back on the jet, they had been offered a drink. Chet and Rosario asked for water. Ivan had a rum and coke.

"I don't think they want us drunk," Rosario said, standing tall under Ivan's icy glare.

"That's because they don't know what the hell they're sending us into. When this is done, we'll all need to drink until we black out."

Chet checked his pulse a few times, making sure Rosario couldn't see what he was doing. His heart rate was higher than normal, but then again, he was exhausted and on a private jet, racing toward another possible horror show. He was sweating, but again, it had to be from stress, not a fever. His muscles didn't have that dull ache that came from an elevated temperature.

The possibility of some kind of cross species virus transmission was too astronomical for Chet to even consider. Whatever was affecting the orcas was, so far, a strictly orca phenomenon. What he should worry about was it bouncing over to dolphins.

Stop making yourself nuts!

If exposure to the orcas was the catalyst, all three of them should be showing some kind of symptoms by now. Chet's exhausted mind had become his worst enemy. He knew it deep down in his heart and this had to stop. He went to the bathroom, splashed water on his face and settled down.

"You are not sick. You…are not…sick."

Only once he felt more in control of himself did he go back into the cabin. Rosario and Ivan were asleep. He joined them, getting in forty restless minutes.

It was just an hour before daybreak when they circled the oil rig. They leaned to the left of the helicopter to see the madness below.

"Dear God," Rosario whispered.

If they didn't know better, they'd swear that the rig was caught in the middle of a terrific storm, the seas kicked up to a heady froth.

"How many can there be?" Chet said, watching a seemingly endless stream of orcas batter every support holding the rig up.

Ivan's breath was foul as it wafted over Chet's shoulder. "It looks like every goddamn orca in the Atlantic."

The helicopter touched down on the landing pad. Chet wasn't sure he wanted to get off.

As his foot reached solid ground, he could feel the steady reverberations of the orca bodies slamming into the rig. It felt like the whole thing was going to collapse at any second.

He looked back at the helicopter with a wistful gaze. Before he could change his mind, grab Rosario and jump back inside, it took off.

"Why do I feel like we've been left to die?" he said.

Rosario clutched his arm as the solid steel of the rig made noises that did little to instill confidence in its structural integrity.

Tough looking men and women lined the sides of the platform, staring down. With very few exceptions, the word *ashen* best described their faces.

A heavyset man with a sharp crew cut and squinty eyes speed walked to them.

"You the fella from the aquarium?" he asked, extending his hand.

Chet saw Ivan's jaw muscles flex, but he bit his tongue. The man hated when people called Marine Paradise an aquarium. "Ivan Padron. This is Chet Clarke and Rosario Benitez. They were present when we had our...issue."

Handshakes went all around. "I'm John Rafferty. I don't know if you're just in time or too late."

"Meaning what?" Ivan said.

"Come with me."

The rig was lit up so it was bright as day, long shadows stretching out before them as they stayed close to Rafferty. He stopped at the east corner of the rig. A dozen men were gathered at the rail.

And they were holding guns.

"What the hell do they think they're doing?" Chet exclaimed.

"Saving our lives," Rafferty said, his small eyes boring into Chet's.

"Tell them to back off," Ivan said.

The rig shuddered as if it had been body slammed by a ninety-foot blue whale.

"We don't have time," Rafferty said.

Ivan turned on him with fire in his eyes. "I didn't come here to watch a bunch of roughnecks slaughter orcas. Tell them to hold their fire and back the hell away!"

Rafferty was stunned, obviously not at all used to being spoken to like that. He sneered at Ivan who sneered right back. After a tense minute, Rafferty exhaled and barked at his men to step back...for the moment.

Chet, Rosario and Ivan hustled through the crush of beefy bodies. None of the men looked pleased to have their game of shooting fish in a barrel called off.

The rig shook and Chet nearly lost his footing. His chest hit hard into the railing.

Now he knew why the men were at this corner.

The rig was being attacked on all sides. The largest concentration of orcas was right below their feet. It was as if they sensed a weakening of the support and were tripling their efforts to exploit it.

"Is it getting tired to keep saying this is impossible?" Chet said.

"It's not, because this is," Rosario said.

There had to be hundreds of orcas at this section of the rig alone. Chet had never even imagined a pod this large. Nor had he ever conceived of so many focused on the destruction of a solitary object. These orcas were not at play. They hammered the rig over and over again, regardless of the harm they were inflicting on themselves. Several spotlights had been concentrated on this side. Under their brutal glare, he saw with revulsion that the water was a deep, dark crimson.

A heavy groan thrummed in the air, the vibration hitting him in the pit of his gut.

"What was that?" Rosario said.

Rafferty shouted above the wounded steel, "That's the sound of your funeral if you don't let my men clear those killer whales out of here."

"You can't just shoot them," Rosario said.

"Better that than watch this whole operation and everyone on it sink into the ocean. You know what will happen, sister? First, the whole thing will go up in a ball of flame that will fry you to a crisp in seconds. If you somehow survive that, the fall will kill you. If you get through that, you have to hope the wreckage doesn't break you in half. And if you said all your hail Mary's and our fathers and somehow survived, I can guarantee you those killer whales will finish what they started. When getting eaten alive is the best you can hope for, you can't just sit with your fingers up your ass."

Rosario lunged at the man. "I'm not your sister, you tub of shit!"

Chet pulled his eyes away from the terrifying spectacle below and restrained her.

Rafferty looked to Ivan. "You got any other ideas?"

Ivan didn't turn to look at him. He stared at the frenzy of orcas with wide eyes. "Why are they here?"

"What did you say?" Rafferty said. His men had started to close in, rifles held close to their barrel chests.

Now Ivan whirled on him. "I can't understand why they're all here. Are you doing something other than drilling for oil? There has to be a goddamn reason."

The oil man spat between his feet. "Are you outta your mind? No, we're not doing anything we haven't done for the past seven years. Were you doing anything strange when your killer whales went ape shit in your little aquarium?"

Chet was sure he'd have to find a way to hold both Ivan and Rosario back from hitting the man. He knew the moment they did, Rafferty's men would be all over them. With tensions running so high, they couldn't expect cooler heads to prevail. These men were toting guns. Things would end badly for the three of them if it got out of hand.

"You can't just kill them," Rosario said, her body like coiled steel in Chet's hands. "They can't control what's happening to them. They're innocent."

"Tell that to the people who died while you watched. I'm sure as shit not going to let that happen here."

Chet finally spoke up. "Or is it more important to make sure AOI's six-hundred-million dollar investment doesn't end up in the bottom of the sea?"

Rafferty signaled for his men to retake their positions. They knocked into Chet and Rosario, steering clear of Ivan.

"Six of one, half a dozen of the other," Rafferty said. "The way I see it, if we get these whales to realize the error of their ways, it's what you call a win-win situation."

Would it matter if he told them there were baby and adolescent orcas down there?

During kills, sometimes, the adults would watch the younger orcas attack their prey, stepping in when needed to give them pointers. They learned first by watching, then by doing. It was utterly amazing how orca pods established training sessions for the next generation. Some would say the ability to teach was human, but in orcas, Chet always felt it was degrading to them to compare them to hairless apes. In so many regards, they were super human.

What was going on below them was no training session. Every orca was involved in the task of destroying the rig.

No, Chet decided, it wouldn't make a lick of difference to Rafferty that so many young orcas were in the frenzy. The man's mind was made up and he had the backing of his entire crew.

In a way, he couldn't blame them. It really felt as if the entire oil rig was about to collapse like a stack of Jenga blocks. Several times, he'd had to find a handhold to keep upright.

"Don't! Don't!" Rosario wailed. Before she could grab the back of a man's collar, Chet pulled her away. He worried, for good reason, that he would turn around and shoot her for trying to stop him. The smell of bloodlust and fear wrapped everyone on the deck in its tangy embrace.

Ivan stood to the side, watching the orcas, a burly man in a wool cap leaning on the rail next to him, his rifle pointed toward the roiling ocean.

"How can you just watch it?" Chet asked.

Ivan's red-rimmed eyes told Chet he hated this as much as them. "Because I have to see how they react. We're not here to look away."

"And we're not here to watch innocent animals get slaughtered," Rosario countered. Ivan cast his eyes back to the violent ocean, visibly ashamed, but in his own way, duty bound.

The sun was just peeking over the horizon when the first shot rang out. It was immediately followed by a cascade of sharp cracks. Everyone on the rig's platform had formed a wall behind Chet. Even if he wanted to get the hell away from the mass murder, he couldn't.

The men kept on firing, some having to pause to reload.

Ivan looked on, unblinking despite the steady thunder from the rifles.

A distant rumbling overhead had Chet looking for storm clouds, but there were none to be seen. He assumed it was his own heartbeat thrumming in his ears.

Chet found he couldn't just stand in the background. He had to see. Squeezing Rosario's hand, he angled around the throng of spectators until they could safely look over the edge.

He looked down, and felt his knees buckle.

CHAPTER TWELVE

The height of the oil rig's platform worked against the efficacy of the rifles. By the time the bullets reached the adult orcas, the damage they inflicted was less than what they had been doing to themselves.

However, the younger orcas didn't have the same protective mass.

By the time the last shot rang out, twenty-three orcas were dead – all of them babies. The pods ceased their attack, the high-pitched cries of their lament giving rise to goosebumps on every single person on the rig. The collective mournful wail of hundreds of orcas would follow everyone who heard it to their graves.

Because of the extreme action taken by Rafferty's men, they would not be heading to those graves today.

Chet and Rosario watched as the pods swam away from the rig, seemingly into the sun itself. The spray from their spouts rained a fine mist on the ocean's surface.

The workers had walked away, gathering in a tight circle around Rafferty. They were too far for Chet to hear what was being said.

"The guns didn't stop them," Ivan said, coming up behind them.

"It sure looked like they did to me," Chet said, massaging his temples.

Ivan looked like he was half with them, half somewhere deep inside his own head. "No. I saw. The orcas weren't slowing down, no matter how many bullets were coming down on them. With the way they were hurting themselves, I'm not sure they could have even noticed they were being shot."

"You forget I saw it, too," Rosario said. "Once they realized their babies were being killed, they pulled back." She looked like she wanted to run over and rip Rafferty's throat out with her teeth. Chet was feeling pretty much the same.

"I'm telling you, that wasn't it. We won't know if the bullets even killed them. I'll bet most of them died from self-inflicted wounds. They could have been dead all along, but we couldn't see them through the scrum. I don't think we're going to get any assistance to save a few for a field autopsy." Ivan kicked at the rail. "It was something else. One second they were working in tandem to destroy the rig, the next," he snapped his fingers, "they stop and swim away. No, it wasn't Rafferty's men. It was something else."

Chet sighed. "That's all well and good, but it means nothing if we can't figure out what that something else was. And they damn well better help us save some of those bodies. Why else would we even be here?"

His anger and adrenaline were bleeding away fast, making way for bone crushing fatigue to come crawling back.

"No one's going in that water," Rosario said. "At least not until we know for sure the orcas are truly gone. I don't want them to get hurt, but I can't trust them either."

Many of the bodies were already sinking, carried by the tide and out of sight. So much valuable data, lost.

Chet turned his back to the railing and sank down onto his ass, staring at the men around Rafferty. There were no cheers that they had saved the oil rig. Chet saw the horror on their faces once they stopped shooting, the baby orcas bleeding out and turning onto their sides, filling their lungs with water.

Could Ivan be right?

Chet didn't watch the entire time, but he did see that the bullets weren't slowing the orcas down one iota. It was as if a switch had been flipped. As a single unit, they stopped thrashing around, turning to join the pods clustered around the other supports as they headed out to sea.

What in heaven's name could get several hundred orcas to do such a thing? Yes, they had a complex language, but each pod possessed its own dialect. To think that all these different pods speaking variations of the same language could communicate so quickly, so succinctly that not a single one missed the message to cease was unfathomable.

The rhythmic thrumming of a chopper approaching the platform got Chet's attention. Rafferty's huddle broke up, a few people walking with him to the helipad.

"Looks like the big cheese is here," Ivan said.

"Maybe he'll give us the resources to save at least one orca body," Chet said, too tired to stand. Rosario stood next to him, arms folded across her chest.

"Just let him know that there are thousands of orcas in the Atlantic to his dozens of offshore oil rigs," Ivan said. "I'm sure he'll give us whatever we want."

When the news broke about Portugal, Jamel was watching an old episode of *All in the Family*, fighting insomnia. After a lifetime of sleep issues, he wasn't the least bit fazed by a sleepless night. That just meant more caffeine to get through the day. Until his first cup of coffee, he was happy to sit in his ratty chair, riding the wave of a semi-daze.

The station's programming of seventies sitcoms in need of a remastering gave way to the early edition of the local news. The story about a horde of killer whales attacking an AOI oil rig along the southern coast of Portugal snapped Jamel to full attention. He pushed the blanket off, bending forward so he was closer to the TV, as if it made any difference.

The female anchor, Maisy Goodfellow, had been a staple of the morning airwaves. The middle-aged Inuit still had her striking good looks, though her body had gotten noticeably matronly over the years.

"Engineers from American Oil Industries are currently assessing the damage done to the platform's supports. All operations have been put on hold until they can confirm that the structure hasn't been compromised. It's estimated that upwards of three hundred killer whales descended on the oil rig in the early hours of the morning. After using their bodies to ram the supports for several hours, they suddenly stopped, heading west, away from the AOI's oil rig. No word yet on what attracted them in the first place."

Her partner du jour, a silver haired man who had been transferred from some station in the lower forty-eight shook his head at Maisy.

"Three hundred killer whales," he said in his polished anchor voice, which sounded about as insincere as it could possibly get. "That doesn't seem possible."

Maisy Goodfellow looked genuinely rattled. "We hope to have a marine biologist on during the eight o'clock hour. Hopefully they can shed some light on this truly strange behavior." Before they could segue to a commercial, she said just above a whisper, "I can't imagine what the people on that rig must have been feeling."

Silver hair went into phony smile mode, looked into the camera and announced, "After the break, why bacon can actually be good for you. And we'll have a follow up story on the single mother of quintuplets and her quest to find the man who left her a mother of multiples. Spend your morning with us."

Jamel dug into the chair's cushion to find the remote. He just caught the tail end of the same story on a national news program. This one had a video of the oil rig, but it could have been old or stock footage for all he knew.

Running across the cold floor in bare feet, he grabbed his laptop and sat on the bed. A quick search pulled up a whole page of stories about the latest orca attack. Details were sketchy this early on. He suspected AOI was doing its best to keep things quiet.

"I'll bet one of your employees on the rig spilled the beans."

Living in Alaska, he was well versed in the oil industry, especially its lure of good money for honest work. In just a few months stint, a man could make enough to keep him in jerky and beer for two years.

Networks paid good money, too, especially for stories that built on previous ones.

Scrolling through the different websites, Jamel spotted one from some news organization he never heard of (*must be Portuguese*, he thought) that had some actual pictures. They weren't the best quality, but good enough to make out what was going on.

One showed two small killer whales on their backs, their white bellies exposed to the sun. Blood looked to be spilling from the head of one. Another shot caught the incredible number of spouts in the distance. It was grainy as hell, but terrifying.

How could there be so many?

Jamel didn't even think there were that many killer whales alive in the whole world. Weren't they an endangered species?

Reaching for a pad of paper and a pen, he made a note to do some research on killer whales. What he knew about them could fill a shot glass.

He sure as hell was motivated to learn about them now.

Two more pictures showed the chaos on the deck of the rig.

In one of them, a man and woman stood close to one another, staring daggers at the men walking away.

"You look familiar."

Opening another window, Jamel went to his bookmarks folder and clicked the link to the story about the killer whale attack at the marine park in Spain.

Coming out of the park were the same man and woman. They were identified as Chet Clarke and Rosario Benitez, a marine biologist and his assistant from the U.S. who had come to be present for the birth of a new calf. Naturally, that birth never happened.

"But something else was born there," Jamel said, forgetting to blink.

Two seemingly targeted attacks in the same sector of the world.

Nah, that couldn't be a coincidence.

He headed to the kitchen to fire up a pot of coffee. Then he sat down at what he liked to call his command center, which was just a corner of his living room with his desktop computer that he'd built himself and stacks of books and bursting file folders.

This is where he did most of his research on a topic that had gotten its hooks in him ten years ago. It was the reason he'd come to live in Alaska in the first place. Hell, he'd basically lived undercover for two years, though he didn't work for any spy agency. His mother used to chide him that he would get his ass into hot water for prying into people's business. He couldn't help being born with a burning curiosity. The problem really came when he dug too deep into things, and then exposed his findings to anyone who would listen to him.

It was borderline cute when he was little, but now, as an adult keeping tabs on things his and other governments desperately wanted to keep secret, it could be deadly.

But the world was changing, and the veils of secrecy were dropping one by one.

There was definitely something going on when it came to the sea. The prehistoric chimera fish, or ghost sharks, that had exploded from their frozen methane prison in the depths of the Atlantic Ocean a few years ago had shown the world that man didn't know everything. Dinosaurs may not walk the Earth (or perhaps they did), but they did still exist in the murky depths of our oceans.

Then there was the whole revelation at Loch Ness, where a horde of strange creatures had been slain when they rose up to attack everyone on land and water. The monster was real, and it was unlike anything anyone had ever dreamed. Scientists were still studying the bodies and attempting to classify the strange creatures.

However, despite whistle blowers like WikiLeaks, twenty-four hour news cycles, revelations of unexplainable creatures and a steady stream of information, there were still dark parts of the globe. Jamel was going to shine the light onto them, no matter what it took.

Killer whales were no strangers to mankind, but their escalating violent behavior appeared to him to be a tipping of the hand by a shadow force intent in preying on man's newfound fear of what lurks beneath the waters.

Keep everyone afraid, Jamel thought.

It was the mindset of all terrorists.

And now that fear was spreading all the way to Europe, just as he knew it would.

Except he'd never planned for this.

CHAPTER THIRTEEN

It took some convincing with the executive vice president of AOI's European operations, but he eventually relented and had his men retrieve one of the orca corpses. Convincing actually meant Ivan threatening to tell the whole world that his men shot and killed baby orcas. No matter how justified it may have been, the world would come crashing down on AOI if word got out, and they didn't want that.

For a while there while Ivan was shouting at the man, Chet worried that the bespectacled executive would simply have the Spaniard tossed overboard. Stakes were high. What was one life compared to billions of dollars that could potentially be lost?

You're getting jaded in your old age, Chet admonished himself.

Chet, Rosario and Ivan had to go down to the whale, as there was no way to bring it up to the main deck. Together, they did what they could with the tools they had at their disposal. Flocks of seagulls cawed incessantly overhead, waiting for the humans to be done with the carcass.

Mostly they gathered blood and tissue samples, along with a sizeable chunk of the orca's brain. When they were finished, the scavenger birds lit upon the baby whale, tearing it to bits as it floated away from the rig.

By the time they made it back topside, there was a non-disclosure agreement waiting for them. They were to report any findings to AOI, but not talk to anyone about what had happened. Basically, they had never been there.

"I have to have this analyzed by my marine tech," Ivan grumbled, indicating the pile of bags at their feet.

The executive, with Rafferty by his side, took out his tablet and said, "I'll need their name and address so I can have a document sent to them as well."

As much as Chet wanted to tell the man to cram his NDA up his one-percenter ass, he knew they weren't getting off this rig without signing. They stepped away from the oil men to discuss.

"I'm too tired to argue," Rosario said.

"That's exactly what he counted on," Ivan said.

Chet rolled his neck, bones cracking. "I agree, but I also don't want to spend the rest of my life out here."

"They can't kidnap us," Ivan said.

They looked back at Rafferty and his men. One of them had found his rifle again. He made a big point out of casually looking at it, lovingly running his hand along the stock.

"No, they can do much worse," Chet said. "I think this time, we gotta let the Wookie win."

"I fucking hate this," Ivan said with a sneer that would have made Elvis envious.

Chet patted his back. "Live to fight another day."

The moment they signed their NDAs, they were helped into a waiting helicopter along with their sample bags. Expecting to have to fly coach back to Spain, they were surprised when they were escorted onto the same private jet. And this time, there was top shelf booze made available to them. Ivan was more than happy to take advantage of some Glenmorangie Pride 1981 single malt scotch.

"How much is a bottle of this stuff worth?" he asked the pretty flight attendant.

"I believe a little over four thousand U.S.," she replied.

"It's worth every penny," he said, settling into the plush leather seat.

Rosario declined a drink while Chet asked for a simple beer.

"I already feel like a whore," Rosario said.

Ivan knocked back the scotch, shaking his glass for more. "Don't knock whores. If they keep off the drugs, they can live like queens."

By the time the plane reached altitude, all three of them had fallen asleep.

Chet hadn't realized until they'd gotten back to the hotel that he'd left his cell phone behind. He checked to see a slew of messages. There were the usual from his mother and his friend Mike. And then there were a bunch of calls from a number and area code he didn't recognize.

Moving over to voicemail, the computerized female voice announced, "You have ten new messages."

"And no desire to listen to a single one of them."

He plugged it in to charge and left it on the desk.

He slipped down to the hotel's gift shop and bought a thermometer. He hadn't felt sick or feverish since being on the jet headed toward the oil rig, but he wanted to be sure. Knowing he looked silly sitting in the lobby with a thermometer in his mouth, he did it just the same.

"Normal," he said, reading where the mercury had stopped. "Not that anything has been normal."

The episodes of panic were nothing more than the one-two punch of stress and exhaustion. Chet was pretty sure no one would admonish him for it. They didn't know what the hell they were dealing with here. It could be anything.

But it's not a virus that can jump from orcas to man, he reminded himself.

What worried him most was that if he got panicky, a man who was a professional, what would become of others? A mass panic could be on the horizon, and that might end up being worse than the enraged orcas.

Stepping back into the room, he looked into the open bathroom door.

Rosario had stripped off all her clothes and was running the shower. God, even after living through the nightmare of the past few days, she looked gorgeous. The nap on the plane had done him some good. He felt a definite tightening of his boxers.

"I need to wash everything off me," she said.

Down boy, he ordered his crotch.

"Keep the water on when you're done," he said.

He knew they reeked of dead orca based on the looks they had gotten from people in the airport and hotel. Chet had sadly become used to it.

A weak smile played at the corners of Rosario's full lips. "I don't know. I think it's best if we conserve water."

She turned to step into the shower. The sight of her firm ass had Chet out of his clothes in record time.

Under a scalding hot spray, they ground against one another as if fucking were the only way to exorcise the madness and death that had entered their lives. By the time they were done, the water had gone cold and they were red and tender in more places than they could count.

When his cell phone rang at three in the morning, Chet snapped wide awake.

So did Rosario.

"Who is it?" she asked, trying to look over his shoulder at the phone.

Chet had expected it to be Ivan again. Thankfully, it wasn't.

"It's someone from The Dolphin Experience in Fort Meyers. Guess they have a job for me. You'd think they could call at a decent hour."

Rosario crashed back into the pillows. "They don't know you're in Spain. It's nine in the morning there."

"Oh, yeah. I keep forgetting the time zones. My brain is fried."

He was tempted to swipe the call into voicemail.

Going against his better, exhausted judgment, he answered instead.

"Hello, this is Chet."

"Thank God," the woman replied, breathing heavily into the phone. "Chet, it's Ann-Marie Smalls from The Dolphin Experience."

Chet sat up straighter. "What's going on? You sound upset."

"We…we just had an incident. One of our trainers went in to feed Naala and, well…he was attacked."

"Is he all right?"

A line of sweat broke out along Chet's spine.

He'd delivered Naala eight years ago. Her parents had since passed away. Chet had always had a special affection for Naala, who was one of the most tender, loving orcas he'd ever encountered.

Of all the orcas in the world, he'd never expect something like this to happen with Naala. Never.

If she wasn't impervious to whatever was happening to the orca population, none of them were.

"He's dead. The moment he stepped onto the platform, Naala jumped up and grabbed him. By the time we got there, he...he...he was in two pieces."

Ann-Marie sounded on the brink of tears.

"We can't even get him out of the water, Chet. Naala, she's gone crazy. You should see her. We tried to tranquilize her, but kept missing. We've run out of supplies."

Rosario, sensing more shit was hitting the fan, was now up and leaning against Chet so she could hear the other end of the line.

Chet thought he'd be numb to news like this by now, but he was wrong. "I'll call Ocean World and have them send over Robert, discreetly, of course. He'll be able to get Naala down."

The Dolphin Experience and Ocean World were rivals, but considering what was going on lately, Chet was pretty sure Robert, their full time marine biologist, wouldn't flinch at trying to help.

Jesus, Chet thought, *what if Ocean World was experiencing the same thing? What if all of the orcas in all the parks have suddenly gone mad, just like the orcas at the oil rig? What the fuck is behind all of this? Some kind of pandemic? A change in the Earth's electromagnetic field? Radiation from space?*

Nothing seemed too ludicrous at this point.

"Chet, is there any chance you can get here soon?" Ann-Marie asked.

He sighed, exasperated and helpless. "I'm in Barcelona right now. I'll start looking for flights home, but it's going to take some time."

"You weren't there for the incident at Marine Paradise, were you?"

"That, and more. I'll tell you when I see you. Just hold tight. Do not let anyone near Naala's tank other than Robert."

"I won't."

Chet hung up and called Ocean World. He got ahold of Barry Zucco, whom he'd known for going on ten years. Barry was in no better shape than Ann-Marie. By the time Chet disconnected the call, he felt hollowed out.

Rosario gripped his arm. "Chet, what's going on?"

"It's happening in Ocean World, too. Their two orcas have flipped out. Luckily, no one was hurt. But they're displaying aggressive behavior. They'll send Robert to The Dolphin Experience when and if he can get their situation under control."

His fingers clenched so hard, it hurt. Or it should have if he wasn't feeling as if he were having an out of body experience.

"How?" she sputtered.

"I have to make a call."

Going to his contacts file, he hit call on the number for Green Gardens in Connecticut, the only other park on the east coast that had a captive orca. After several transfers, he finally got the park's chief of operations on the line.

It was a big relief to hear that their orca, Keanu, was fine. Chet explained what had happened in Florida and made the man promise to cancel the day's shows and keep all personnel clear of Keanu's tank.

When he was done, he ran across the room and fired up his laptop, looking for flights to Florida. Rosario started packing before putting on her clothes.

Chet's heart was in his throat, fearing that this was just the beginning of something far, far worse to come.

CHAPTER FOURTEEN

The last minute flight from Barcelona to Orlando was expensive, but Chet didn't care. Marine Paradise had already agreed to pay for his flight home, which had been scheduled for the following day. Chet didn't mind paying the extra fee. He was desperate to get to Florida.

They landed thirteen hours and several time zone changes later. He and Rosario had made it a point to grab as much sleep and eat as much terrible food on the plane as possible so they were somewhat refreshed as they deplaned.

Stepping out of Orlando International Airport to get a taxi, Rosario fanned her face. "Why do people choose to live here? It's literally hotter than hell."

"They stay indoors with their air conditioners from late May until late September. Although, if you're on blood thinners, this place is paradise."

"This kind of heat and humidity is not fit for human consumption." Rosario pulled her shirt away from her chest, which then caught the eye of the man in charge of getting rides for the waiting passengers. They had a car waiting for them in record time.

"Nice work," Chet said, loading their bags in the trunk.

"What?" Rosario said as she slipped in the car.

"Huh? Nothing."

She was sexy without even being aware of it. Score another in the win column. Chet worried that their relationship would be intrinsically tied in with the string of calamities they had gone through. Once everything went back to normal, would it be the same? Would she move on to greener, saner pastures?

Sitting in the back seat, he rubbed his face and willed his budding relationship paranoia to go away. He had far bigger things to worry about.

The park was closed by the time they pulled up to the gate. Chet told the attendant they were there to see Ann-Marie Smalls.

After a quick call, they were allowed inside. Chet paid the driver and gathered their bags.

Ann-Marie met them at the entrance to the dolphin exhibit. She looked utterly worn out. Her last name was Smalls and she lived up to it. The cherry-blonde woman barely hit five feet.

"Naala is sedated," she said after he introduced her to Rosario. "Robert made it here a couple of hours after I spoke to you. We've had police and news crews here all day. In fact, you just missed them. I know the reporters will be back in time for the ten o'clock news."

"We've had our share of them lately," Chet said.

"Not to mention orca attacks," Rosario said.

Ann-Marie motioned for them to follow her. "I'll take you to Naala."

The orca slowly swam around the tank, coming up for air in steady intervals. She was calm but not under, which was a good thing. Keeping a safe distance, Chet's heart broke.

"They want us to put her down for good," Ann-Marie said.

Whenever there was an orca attack, a sector of the public called for it to be euthanized. Animal rights activists would shout them down, railing against a system that allowed such wonderful and wild creatures to have been captured in the first place.

In the past, orcas that had turned on their handlers were either put into a kind of solitary confinement, which to Chet was worse than death, or shipped off to another marine park to be someone else's problem. Neither solution was acceptable as far as he was concerned.

"Poor girl," Rosario said.

Naala's dorsal fin was bent over, a common trait of captive orcas. In the wild, dorsal fins were always tall and straight, some reaching over one meter high. If they did have a collapsed dorsal fin, it was a sign they were sick or injured.

Everyone who worked with orcas knew that man had yet to devise the perfect living environment for them. The fin was an outward sign of their abnormal inner health, discontent and in many cases, depression.

"Who was the handler?" Chet asked.

Fresh tears brimmed in Ann-Marie's eyes. "Matthew."

Chet clutched the rail in front of him. He knew Matthew well. He was a great guy, just under thirty with a wife and twin baby girls. Matthew and Naala were inseparable.

Now, they couldn't be further from one another.

"How did his family take it?"

"As good as can be expected. Surprisingly, they don't want any harm to come to Naala."

Chet nodded. "I'm sure through Matthew, they understood the kind of work we do. To the public, it looks fun and sometimes magical. But it's delicate and dangerous, usually more so for the orcas than the people, but…but…"

He lost his train of thought, eyes locked on a slumbering Naala.

"How do you think she'll be when she wakes up?" Rosario said.

"I don't know, but I want to make sure we're here when that happens. We didn't get that chance at Marine Paradise. Maybe it'll be like the pods in Portugal and she'll just carry on as if nothing happened."

Sighing, Rosario said, "That's almost worse. You'd like to see some consistent change in behavior so we can get a handle on this."

"Are you going to Ocean World?" Ann-Marie asked.

"Tomorrow," Chet replied. "I'm sure Robert has things under control there. I want to be here for Naala now."

It would be another thirty minutes until the sun would set. The humidity had dropped just enough to take the edge off the stifling heat. Pretty soon, the lights would be turned on so they could keep an eye on Naala.

"I'll get us some coffee," Ann-Marie said.

Jamel had called in sick to work and was existing on Red Bulls and licorice. Ever since the madness at the oil rig, he'd devoted all his time to searching for other anomalous incidents involving sea mammals.

He didn't have long to wait. Two Florida parks had seen their killer whales go berserk as well. Luckily, this time there was only one fatality, though one was still too much.

He tried getting in touch with Sam, but she wasn't around.

That guy, Chet Clarke, hadn't returned any of his calls.

Probably because he thinks you're a nut, Jamel thought. *I shouldn't have left so many messages. But at least I didn't spill all the beans. No one could handle that, especially over voicemail.*

Sitting in his command center, he stared at his cell phone, contemplating whether he should call the marine biologist again. Was he in Florida now? Or could he still be at that oil rig in Portugal? If he was in Europe, there was a chance he hadn't heard about the killer whale incidents in Florida.

If Jamel kept calling, a total stranger from the wilds of Alaska, would the man just block his number? God knows Jamel would if the roles were reversed.

If and when he did get through to Chet, would he just hang up the moment Jamel explained why he thought the killer whales were going crazy?

Yep, odds are he would.

Life wasn't easy when you were one of the few people who knew what the hell was really going on and the powers that be had brainwashed the entire world to laugh at anyone who caught even a whiff of the truth.

He checked a satellite map, zeroing in on Kalach, a remote town in the Urals of Russia. A former logging town, Kalach was reported to be just a handful of hearty residents away from being a ghost town. Several articles with pictures of snow swept landscapes and weathered people could easily be found on the Web. Kalach was almost a forgotten footnote in history. Until that time, it was an interesting slice of life piece for news outlets when they needed filler.

LOYAL TO THE END. WEATHERED PEOPLE OF KALACH REFUSE TO LEAVE THEIR BELOVED HOMES.

Jamel knew better.

Those people in the photos weren't real.

Well, they were real people, but they didn't live in Kalach.

Yes, the town had been abandoned, but something else had been quietly installed ten years ago. Kalach was far from prying eyes, a perfect place for this little slice of Russian experimentation. The articles on the death of Kalach were designed to keep people away.

What better place to hide something than in plain sight?

He'd tacked up a picture he had of the antenna array on his wall. It had been captured by a passing satellite and quickly taken down. Not quick enough for Jamel to have saved the file, making several copies.

To the uninitiated, the squared-off clearing in the woods of Kalach, crammed with tall metal works, looked very much like a power station.

Oh, there was power there, but it wasn't in place to charge the few remaining light bulbs in the dying town.

Those steel towers were, collectively, some of the most powerful weapons in the world.

Their use had been steadily increasing over the years, altering the world in small ways here and there.

It looked like the Russians were building up to something bigger and badder.

Knowledge was power…until you came across something like this. Even if Jamel could convince Chet what was behind the orca attacks, would it make a lick of difference?

He popped another Red Bull open, dipping a red licorice stick in it and chewing on the end.

This might be for nothing, but he damn sure wasn't going to just sit around.

Jamel picked up his cell phone and hit redial.

Chet wasn't sure whether he should feel grateful or disappointed that Naala seemed just like her old self in the morning. He, Rosario and Ann-Marie had taken turns napping in the uncomfortable hardback seats of the arena through the night.

Rosario nudged Ann-Marie awake.

"She seems perfectly fine, but I don't know her like you do."

Ann-Marie rubbed her knuckles into her eyes. Her phone had gone off constantly ever since they got there. Around midnight, she'd finally set it to mute. She looked at Naala doing laps in the pool, then her phone, which made her eyes go wide.

"It looks like half the country tried to reach me," she said, whistling a stream of aggravation through her teeth. Tucking the phone into her back pocket, she stood up to get a better look at Naala. "She's definitely calmer than she was yesterday morning. The moment Matthew came in to check on her, she was agitated."

Moving closer, Chet looked for any telltale signs that all was not right with the orca. As she passed by, she caught his eye and he would swear on a tower of Bibles that she not only recognized him, but smiled. His gaze moved past her to the blood stain that had been missed in the corner of the deck.

What did that smile mean?

Was it a knowing look, one that dared him to assume that all was well?

Or was it just amiable Naala, happy to see him?

"She's got to be starving by now," he said. It was just past seven in the morning and already his clothes were sticking to him. He pulled his shirt over his head and dropped it on an empty seat.

"Chet, what do you think you're doing?" Rosario said, rising from her seat.

He looked back at her and saw the worry lines at the corners of her mouth and eyes. She knew exactly what he had in mind. "I'm going to feed her. We can't just let her starve."

"I understand that, but we're going to have to find a safe way to do that first."

He took a deep breath, the humid air coating his lungs with moisture that made him cough. "I'll be careful."

Rosario shook her head violently. "You can't go in there and be careful enough."

"The other attacks went south in a hurry because people were taken by surprise. I need to see how she really is now and I can't do that by throwing fish at her from fifty feet away."

She angled past Ann-Marie. "Then I'm coming with…"

He held up a hand. "No, you're not. Not this time. I need you nearby just in case…I just need you safe."

They stared at one another, Chet trying to look as resolute as he possibly could, despite having some extreme misgivings about his plan. Rosario was on the verge of telling him to shove his macho act up his ass, he just knew it, at least until Ann-Marie touched her hand.

"We'll come get you the second anything happens," Ann-Marie said.

A silent conversation passed between Rosario and Ann-Marie, two women who hardly knew each other. Chet had no idea what was going on telepathically between them, but he was grateful when Rosario exhaled and closed her eyes.

"You have the keys?" he asked Ann-Marie. She flipped a key ring down to him.

"It's the one with the green plastic ring around it."

Eyeing Naala as he walked past the tank at a good distance, he opened up the supply room lined with freezers and refrigerators filled with fish. He grabbed a clean silver bucket and filled it with frozen herring. Normally, the trainers came in early and prepped the copious amounts of freshly delivered fish to be fed to the orcas throughout the day. The delivery most likely wasn't making it today. The Dolphin Experience, just like Marine Paradise and Ocean World, wasn't going to be admitting anyone anytime soon.

Striding back into the warm sunlight, Rosario called out, "Do not take your eyes off her!"

"I won't."

He meant it.

The bucket clipped the gate as he walked onto the deck of the main tank, sounding like a dinner bell. Naala caught the sound, zooming toward him. Her bent dorsal fin plowed through the water, a heavy wave spilling over the edge and pooling around his feet.

Chet's body went stiff as iron, the heavy bucket suddenly weightless in his hand.

Naala was coming, and he didn't know if it was for him or the food.

CHAPTER FIFTEEN

Rosario screamed, "Get out of there!"

Ann-Marie blurted something Chet couldn't understand.

He was rooted to the spot, waiting for Naala to come leaping out of the tank. Only now did he realize how incredibly foolish his plan had been. Naala was young and exceedingly fast. If she wanted to momentarily beach herself and grab him, she could do it before he even had time to pivot and face the exit.

Run! Don't just stand there! Run you fucking idiot!

His body betrayed his brain's commands.

More water was displaced from the tank. Any second now, her massive black and white body would burst over the edge of the pool, several tons of death racing at him like a missile with a grudge.

Chet couldn't breathe. He wasn't sure his heart was even beating. Aside from his panicked thoughts, there was a stillness in his body that scared him more than anything. It was as if he had died and his mind just hadn't caught on.

For some odd reason, he thought about the day he'd bought his first car, a clunker from a shady car dealer who should have paid *him* to take it off the lot. He'd wanted to save up to buy the classic 1972 Plymouth Barracuda, but getting a job delivering pizzas meant he needed a car right away. The Nissan Sentra looked and smelled like it had been in a fire. Every part of it was in deep decay except the motor. Somehow, it had survived five months of zipping around town, the stench of burnt foam, fabric and plastic replaced with savory pizza and meatball subs.

He hadn't lost his virginity in the Sentra, nor had there been any great memories of joy rides with his friends. Together, they fed the town. That was it.

"Naala, please," he heard someone say, realizing it was himself.

Grim certainty turned to shock when he spied her body swimming away from him just under the water's surface. She leaped into the air, landing on her side and diving.

It's what Naala always did when it was time to eat. He called it her Happy Yum Yum Dance. She liked to play around and act silly at feeding time.

That instant of knowing she was not going to kill him brought him crashing back into his body. The weight of the bucket suddenly made his fingers ache and his heart seemed to pump deeper, harder, to make up for lost time. It took him a moment to catch his breath.

He dared take his eyes off Naala to glance back at Rosario and Ann-Marie. Both women had their mouths covered with their hands, the look of terror still plastered all over their faces.

Legs unsteady, he managed to shamble toward the edge of the platform.

Reaching down, his fingers wrapped around an icy cod. He held it up for Naala to see.

She responded by swimming toward him.

Chet tossed the fish into the pool. Naala leapt up and snatched it out of the air, just like a dog catching a Frisbee. She turned and headed for the other side of the tank so she could make another circuit, knowing he'd have more fish at the ready.

They kept at it until the bucket was empty. He filled another, and when that one was done, she stopped and floated by the edge, waiting for him to pat her head like he and Matthew always did.

"I'm sorry Naala, not today," he said, feeling awful for denying her that small bit of contact and comfort.

He couldn't chance it. Not yet.

When he was done, he was nearly knocked over from Rosario rushing into him.

She kissed him long and hard. "You're insane, you know that?" she said.

"I know. But at least Naala isn't, at least at the moment."

Ann-Marie looked both happy and pissed.

"That's the last crazy ass stunt you pull," she said, then getting on the tips of her toes to clutch his shoulders. "Naala will be fed from a safe distance from here on."

"She's not a betta fish," Chet said. "She's going to need attention and affection. You know what happens when orcas don't get that."

Ann-Marie sighed, exasperated. "What else can I do? She killed Matthew. I can't have other trainers go in there with her. You know the protocol."

He looked at Naala swimming around as if yesterday hadn't happened. "I think our protocols suck."

"You and me both, but for now, there's not much else I can do. Come on, let me take you to your hotel."

Rosario gave a short laugh. "We didn't even have time to book one."

"That's all right. I'll get you some breakfast then book you in the Hyatt. Chet, I'll need you back this afternoon. We'll have to run some tests on Naala."

"Yeah." That meant they'd have to tranquilize her once again. He wasn't looking forward to it.

On the ride to the Waffle House, which had been Rosario's selection since she'd heard so much about the hash browns but had never been there, Chet finally checked his phone messages.

When he got to the third voicemail from a guy named Jamel Abrams he was tempted to turn the phone off.

"I know you'll probably delete this, but please, hear me out," the man said as if he could read Chet's mind. "I think I've pinpointed what's making all these killer whales lash out and where it's coming from. I can't go into specifics over voicemail. It's better if we talk. I'm sure you'll have lots of questions. Luckily, I have lots of answers."

His head resting against the passenger side window, Chet reluctantly saved the message, only to find four more similar messages from Jamel Abrams. He showed the number to Rosario.

"You know where that area code's from?"

"907? No idea. Why?"

"Alaska," Ann-Marie said, turning into the Waffle House parking lot.

When she noticed Rosario staring at her with a slightly open mouth, she added, "I worked for the phone company for five years. Some things you never forget, try as you might."

Emerging from the car, Chet felt the sun warming the top of his head. "You guys go inside. I just need to make a quick call."

"Should I order you anything?" Rosario asked.

"Coffee and a waffle with bananas."

"No hash browns?"

"You'll learn the difference between famous and infamous after you've had yours."

She waved him off and followed Ann-Marie inside. The girl had a cast iron stomach.

Chet found Jamel's last call and hit dial. The Alaskan answered on the second ring.

"Who is this?" he said, sounding less than inviting.

Uh-oh, you should have just left well enough alone, Chet thought, second guessing himself and ready to end the call.

"You...you left me a message. Well, actually, a bunch of them."

"Chet Clarke!" Jamel's tone shifted dramatically, now sounding like a long lost friend. "Wow, man, I'm so glad you called. I was afraid I might have scared you off."

"You still might."

"I hear you. And I apologize. Can I call you right back?"

Chet rolled his eyes. The guy leaves him a ton of messages, and when he finally gets the call back he's been asking for, he gives Chet the brush off. What the hell was his game?

"I need to call you on a more secure line is all," Jamel said. "I'll call you in like five seconds."

The call disconnected before Chet could reply. True to Jamel's word, his phone rang a few seconds later.

"Are you sitting down?" Jamel asked.

Chet looked at Rosario and Ann-Marie sipping coffee in the air-conditioned restaurant. He very much wanted to be sitting down.

"I'm fine standing."

"Okay. My next question: have you ever heard of HAARP?"

"As in the instrument?"

"No, it's an acronym for a public yet top secret government program. It stands for the High Frequency Active Auroral Research Program."

Chet pulled the phone away from his ear. How had this lunatic gotten his number?

"That doesn't help," Chet said. "Look, thank you for your concern. We have some very good people looking into this…"

Jamel cut him off. "I worked at HAARP in Alaska for one year. Numerous countries have their own HAARP programs. I know exactly what it's capable of doing, and I know when each array is turned on. Prior to each of the last three killer whale attacks, there's been a spike in output from Russia's installation."

Auroral Research? Arrays? Russians?

It was all too much.

"I've had a long night and people are waiting on me."

"Mr. Clarke? I can tell you when the next killer whale incident is going to happen. I just can't say where. If I give you that, will you at least believe me and talk?"

He almost laughed. After all of the horror and tension of the past few days, a conversation with some government conspiracy nut was an amusing distraction. But he'd had his fill.

"Why not? So, Mr. Abrams, when can we expect the next one?"

He heard the sound of fingers racing across a computer keyboard.

"Shit," Jamel muttered. "You're not even going to need to write this down to remember later. If what I'm seeing is correct, the next one will happen in six to ten hours."

CHAPTER SIXTEEN

While Chet drew blood from a sedated Naala, he asked Rosario to keep an eye on the news on her phone.

"What am I supposed to be on the lookout for?" she asked.

He swept his arms around the medical pool. "The same insanity we've been trapped in all week."

"You don't think…"

"With the way things have been going, anything's possible."

Including Naala suddenly waking up and killing everyone in the pool with her. Ann-Marie had called in ten of her staff to assist Chet with the beloved orca. Chet worked as fast as he could, knowing he still wanted to get over to Ocean World before the day was out.

Exhaustion seemed to be his constant companion lately. Only this time, he wasn't so much worn out from running around than his brain being stuck in overdrive.

All during breakfast, he'd had his head in his phone, researching HAARP. When Rosario asked him what had his attention, he'd told a white lie and said he was checking for any more news coming out of Spain and Portugal.

He learned that HAARP was an atmospheric research facility, the most famous, or infamous if he was to take Jamel Abrams at his word, located in Gakona, Alaska. He'd never heard of Gakona, but he imagined it to be a very remote place, all the better to operate far from prying eyes.

Though approval for HAARP came about in the early nineties, construction wasn't completed until 2007.

Never one to be suckered in by conspiracy theories, he was nevertheless fascinated by the science behind the program. Basically, the HAARP facility contained almost two hundred antennas that were linked to one another and could be rotated. The antennas would push extremely low frequency, or ELF, waves into the ionosphere in order to study their effects. The stated purpose to charging the ionosphere was to find ways to improve communications and navigation systems. As the ionosphere is constantly bombarded by rays from the sun, understanding its greater workings would help scientists build better systems that rely on radio waves bouncing through the atmosphere. At least that was how Chet was able to bottom line it in his non-physicist way.

Chet was surprised to see so much 'grounded' information available about the program. The project directors for HAARP appeared to work very hard to be transparent to the public, even offering up their records and tests to anyone who desired to see them.

By late 2015, the US Air Force had abandoned HAARP, giving the keys to the whole operation to the University of Alaska Fairbanks.

In just a short amount of time, HAARP had managed to birth a considerable number of conspiracies. The most prominent was that it was being used to heat the ionosphere and control weather patterns. This sort of *weather weapon* could be used against warring nations to plunge them into drought, deluge them in rains and superstorms and basically break their infrastructure. HAARP had been blamed for just about every natural disaster of the past ten years, including earthquakes and tsunamis. Worries about the militarization of the technology abounded. Even Congressmen went on the record to voice their concerns about the potential dangers and hidden agenda of those who ran it.

Aside from weather modification, HAARP was also purported to be able to change the Earth's magnetic poles, be responsible for low, incessant hums heard around the globe, alter dimensional reality and last but not least, exert mind control over targeted areas.

That last one was what had Jamel worked into a lather.

Even though the US HAARP array was basically shut down, other countries had developed their own. The one that caused the most concern amongst Jamel's cohorts was located in Russia. Jamel claimed to be able to detect when the Russian HAARP was being powered up. After a year of silence, it had become very, very active over the past few weeks.

Chet's head hurt, the sun not helping as it seared his cheeks.

"You okay?" Rosario asked as he took a seat in the main theater under the shade.

"Just hot. You know what time it is?"

She checked her phone. "It's almost one. You getting hungry?"

"Nah, I think I'll be digesting that waffle until tomorrow."

Rosario patted his arm. "And here I thought I'd hitched my wagon to a real live hero."

"Superman has kryptonite, I have the Waffle House."

They shared a rare laugh, but deep down, he couldn't stop counting the minutes. He desperately wanted Jamel to be wrong. He'd said another orca attack would occur in six to ten hours. That left five more hours until Chet could dismiss the man as a well meaning crackpot.

"I think we've done all we can here," Rosario said. "Even Ann-Marie went home. You want to head over to Ocean World?"

Both parks were closed to the public pending an investigation into the strange string of 'killer whale violence' that was all over the news. Chet knew that several prominent marine biologists were scheduled to arrive at The Dolphin Experience later in the day, as well as Ocean World. None of them knew the orcas personally as Chet had, but they would be lending their expertise to find the driving force behind the rash of attacks.

Word had also gotten out that Chet and Rosario had been present at the two attacks in Europe and were now on the scene in Florida. They'd put their phones on mute after they blew up from interview requests.

All Chet wanted to do was meet with Rob at Marine World, observe the orcas and be in bed by seven, one hour after he'd be secure that Jamel Abrams was dead wrong.

He smiled at Rosario, who looked as radiant as ever. She wasn't sweating, even though she'd been bouncing around the marine park since they got back from the Waffle House.

He'd like to try his best to get her to sweat before his early night.

"Yep, let's hit the road," he said.

He watched Naala as she came more and more to life, giving her a wave before he left. She swam happily, unaware that he wasn't coming back today.

"I wonder if she remembers what she did," Rosario said.

"Barring something that's affecting her brain and blocking her memory, I'm sure she does. The question is, do orcas carry their guilt? I sure as shit hope not. I'd prefer to think that Naala can live the rest of her life without this hanging over her head."

"And free," Rosario added. "More important than anything, that she'll be free to live her life."

Chet slipped his arm around her waist as they walked to the car, wondering if there really could be a future where all of the captive orcas and dolphins were released from their captivity.

He seriously doubted it.

To do so would be an admission that man had been wrong, and as a species, accountability was a dirty word.

They never made it to Ocean World.

Rosario turned the radio on in the rental car, subjecting Chet to the latest Justin Bieber tune. She jiggled in her seat, which lessened some of the pain, then burst into laughter.

"What, you don't like the Beebs?" she said.

"Not in any way, shape or form."

"Good, because neither do I."

She hit the Seek button. The next station that popped up was an all news station. Before she could cruise on past it, the announcer said, "The Navy has been sent to the scene of yet another killer whale attack, this time on a cargo ship making its return voyage from Panama. No word yet on the number of casualties, but the ship has been sending out a distress signal for the past hour and is said to be taking on water. We'll keep you up to date with this latest tragedy on the high seas and interview Professor William Lund, an expert on killer whale behavior."

Chet had to pull over.

"No fucking way."

Rosario had paled. "Why does this keep happening?"

"You don't understand. Back at the Waffle House, I called a man who said he knew why the orcas were lashing out."

"You what? Why didn't you tell me?"

He turned the radio down, angling the air vents toward his face. "Because I thought...no, I *hoped* he was crazy. He told me that there would be another incident today and that it would happen before six o'clock." Chet pointed at the digital clock in the dashboard. "Looks like he was right."

Struggling to understand, Rosario kept pulling and releasing the seatbelt strap across her chest. Chet thought it must have hurt, but she didn't even flinch.

"Wait, so this random guy calls you out of the blue..."

"Not so out of the blue. He saw that I was at the Barcelona and Portugal incidents and looked me up."

She continued as if he hadn't spoken. "And out of everyone in the world, he's the one person who knows what the hell is really going on and when it will happen next. How is this possible?"

Chet hesitated. "I know when I say it out loud, even I'm going to doubt it."

"Try it anyway."

He told her about HAARP and its possible connection to mind control and how the Russians had been heavily invested in that particular functionality. As the words tumbled from his lips, he expected men in big white nets to appear outside his door. He'd go willingly.

The look Rosario gave him didn't make him feel much better about himself.

"How does this guy – you said his name was Jamel Abrams? – know all this?"

"He worked at HAARP, right up until the Navy pulled out."

"Were you able to verify that?"

"Like I said, I thought he was full of crap. I figured nothing would happen today and I could forget all about him and this HAARP craziness."

Rosario turned her body so her knees pressed against the gearshift and her hands were on his thigh.

"He could have just gotten lucky, you know," she said. "It's been happening pretty regularly."

He'd been so caught up in waiting for the other shoe to drop before six that he'd failed to even consider the man had simply won the guessing game.

Chet's phone started to go off, an unrecognized number lighting up on the screen. He swiped it to voicemail. As soon as he did, another call from another unknown number came through.

Rosario patted his thigh. "So, you can choose to ignore this wacko, or we find out if he ever worked at this HAARP thing. Are you going to take that?"

He muted the phone and chucked it in the backseat. "I don't think I'm going to be able to avoid these people much longer. If they dug Professor Lund out of mothballs, reporters are getting desperate for someone who might have some answers."

William Lund was best known for an orca documentary that he'd made thirty years ago, along with its companion book. It was actually a well-made doc that followed a pod of orcas as they traveled from southern California all the way up the North American west coast to Alaska. The man had retired from the University of Miami at least twenty years ago. He thought he'd heard Lund had died. Apparently, the rumors were far from true.

"So what do you want to do now?" Rosario said. Her look told him she was game for whatever path he chose. He cupped her face in his hands and kissed her, both to taste her plump lips and ground himself in reality.

He put the car in drive and merged back onto the road. "First, look up Robert's number at Marine World and call him from your phone. I want to make sure his orcas are still all right. Then, we're going back to the hotel and firing up my laptop. Let's find out who this Jamel Abrams really is."

As they swerved onto the jug handle to take them back to their hotel, Rosario said, "I just thought of something. What if this guy knows so much because he's the one behind it all? He could be like one of those serial killers who plays all kinds of games with the cops, getting off on leading them on a wild goose chase."

Gripping the leather wheel, Chet said, "Despite everything, I have serious doubts this is a manmade issue. Raquel said she should have preliminary lab results by tomorrow. I'm still banking on it being some kind of toxin or new disease. Which then has me worried that it's the start of an orca pandemic. And how far will it spread?"

CHAPTER SEVENTEEN

Chet was no whiz on the computer, at least when it came to searching for someone's history. He could watch videos and look up movie times, maybe download a coupon or two, but that was it. In a generation where computing technology was second nature, Chet was a bit of a throwback. He preferred sticking his nose in nature rather than a digital device.

After a couple of hours of fruitless browsing, he wheeled the chair away from the work desk. Rosario was on the bed trying to find any trace of Jamel Abrams on her tablet.

"You thirsty?" he asked, getting up and stretching.

"Very," she replied, not looking up from the screen.

He opened the hotel fridge and eyed the array of beer and small bottles of hard liquor. A laminated card had been placed on top of the fridge listing the price for each item. Knowing it would be five times more expensive than if he just bought the same things himself, he tossed the card aside.

"What'll it be: beer, whiskey or both?"

"Do they have tequila?"

Chet arched an eyebrow. "Actually, they do. How does Patron suit you?"

"Just fine if you can bring me a beer chaser."

Plucking out the two bottles of tequila, Chet carried them and two cans of Corona to the bed. He dashed to the bathroom and retrieved two glasses, pouring half the bottle of tequila in each.

"I think we've earned this," he said, clinking glasses with Rosario.

"That and a whole lot more," she said, downing the shot. She gingerly placed the glass on the night table, opened a can of Corona and took a deep sip. "That hit the spot."

The peppery sharpness of the tequila made Chet cringe. He'd never been much of a tequila drinker. The cold Corona was a welcome relief.

"You find anything? I've got zilch," he said.

Rosario's finger danced over the screen, closing out several browser windows until she found the one she wanted to show him. It looked to be some kind of site where you could search for people for a fee.

"You said this guy's in Alaska, right?"

"That's what he told me."

"I can't find anyone named Jamel Abrams who is in any way related to the scientific community. And there's no one under that name currently living in Alaska."

"Looks like you and I came crashing into the same wall."

"However, I was able to find a Jamel Abrams who lived in Stamford, Connecticut until five years ago. This guy did spend some time in Juneau, Alaska, where he worked at the University of Alaska Southeast. It appears he was there for one year, living in a rented apartment, and then he went poof."

"Poof?" Chet drained the rest of the beer.

"Vanished."

A chill ran down Chet's spine.

"You mean as in a missing person?"

Rosario took the tiny tequila bottle and polished off the rest, sans glass. "Well, not official as in a police report was opened. It's just that all record of him stops there."

Chet considered his tequila bottle but went to the fridge for some Jack Daniels instead. "Was he a teacher or something?"

"Good question. Let me see."

He watched in amazement as she found the faculty roster of the University of Alaska Southeast, going back several years. "I don't see him listed anywhere. But I did find out that he graduated from Caltech ten years ago. So if this is our guy, he's smart. I would think if a University in Alaska got their hands on a Caltech grad to teach, they would have done some crowing about it."

"So what the hell was he doing up there?"

"Get me another beer and I'll find out."

One hand she used to sip her beer while she used the other to peruse the web, the tablet balanced on her raised thighs. Chet felt a buzz coming on.

While Rosario searched in silence, he dared to look at his phone. He couldn't believe the number of voicemails that had been left in one afternoon. The TV was on with the sound off, locked on a 24-hour news channel. There hadn't been a report about the orcas attacking the freighter for the past thirty minutes. He used to think no news was good news, but he got the feeling that wasn't the case in this instance.

No news could mean the powers that be were blocking anything from coming out. They did say the Navy had dispatched a ship to assist the freighter. If the military told you to keep quiet, you kept quiet, even in this day and age of seemingly unfettered access to news.

"Found him!" Rosario exclaimed. Chet nearly choked on his beer.

He settled next to her on the bed. Her brows were creased with confusion.

"Where did you find him?" he asked.

"I was going through the archives of the college's newspaper. He's mentioned in an article."

"What does it say?"

The light streaming into the room made it hard for him to see anything on the shiny screen.

She angled it towards him. "It appears this Jamel Abrams, who could be your Jamel Abrams, is a custodian."

"A custodian?"

"That whole Caltech thing seems less likely now, doesn't it?"

He scanned the brief article. It was about a rash of vandalism of the school cafeteria. Jamel Abrams was quoted as saying he was going to keep a close eye on it at night to hopefully catch the person or people responsible. There was no accompanying picture.

"What are the odds a janitor has the scoop on top secret Russian ionosphere weapons and how it relates to a high-tech US military facility?" Rosario said.

Chet's stomach clenched. That article blew the theory of Jamel being a scientist right out of the water.

"Slim to goddamn none," he said, dejected.

Rosario tossed the tablet aside. Her eyes were getting glassy from the liquor. "At least you don't have to worry about him anymore."

"Yep, and it only took half a day to realize it."

She straddled his lap, pulling her shirt over her head and slipping off her bra. His hands immediately went to her breasts. "I say we don't waste this little break from insanity," she whispered in his ear. He nibbled on her plump lobe.

When they kissed, he could taste the faint remnants of tequila on her tongue. It tasted a whole lot better this time around.

She had just started working on his belt when someone knocked heavily on the door.

"Mr. Chet Clarke," the voice boomed. "I need to speak with you right away."

Chet thought his ability to be surprised had been burned to the quick, but the sight of two military men outside his hotel room door proved that to be wrong.

He cast a quick look downward to make sure he wasn't sporting a visible bulge in his pants.

"Can I help you?" he said, sounding more confident than he felt.

"Are you Chet Clarke?" one of the men asked. He was in his service dress blues with a white cap. One of Chet's closest friends had been in the Navy. He looked down at the man's sleeve and saw the two stripes and star denoting he was a lieutenant.

"I am."

"We need you to come with us."

Chet gripped the edge of the door.

"Just like that?"

The man's cold green eyes didn't blink. "It's vitally important that you follow me. A car is waiting for us."

There was no sense pretending he didn't know what this was all about. Instead, Chet said, "What's happened with the freighter?"

The man and his companion remained resolute. "We can discuss that in the car."

Chet felt Rosario come up behind him, a light hand on his shoulder.

"How do we know you're who you say you are?" she asked.

"I'd advise you ma'am to look out the window and see for yourself."

Joining her at the window, Chet spotted the black sedan parked in the front of the building. A tan joint light tactical vehicle was idling behind it. The squat but massive jeep on steroids looked like it could plow through a cinderblock wall.

"I don't think they're going to take no for an answer," he whispered.

"They can't kidnap us."

He looked back at the men waiting patiently in the doorway, hands clasped behind their backs.

"To be honest, if they're sending a little entourage, it has to be worse than we've seen so far. I kind of want to know what the hell is going on."

Rosario's eyes narrowed as she peeked around Chet's shoulder. "Okay, but you're not going alone."

Chet smiled. "How did I know you'd say that?"

"Should we pack?' he asked the lieutenant.

"That would be advisable," was his curt reply.

"She's coming with me. I'm not taking no for an answer."

The man didn't even bat an eye. "As you wish. This isn't a shanghai. We just need your help."

They packed quickly. Carrying their bags, Chet had a hard time keeping up with the men. The bags were taken from him and stowed in the trunk of the black Lincoln. The all wheel military vehicle had garnered a lot of attention. Hotel guests lingered outside and in the lobby to see why it was there in the first place. Chet felt uneasy being the center of attention.

"I bet they think we're being pulled in for some sort of interrogation. Or for voting for Trump," he said to Rosario.

"They may not be far off."

The lieutenant held the back door of the Lincoln open for them. Cold air wafted from the dark confines.

"Ladies first," Chet said.

A man was already in the back seat. He was older, his face grave as a funeral director.

"Lieutenant Commander Thomas Wolf," he said, extending his hand to them. "We have a hell of a predicament boiling in the Atlantic. I sure hope you can help."

The man's grip was like a vice. The bones in Chet's hands ground together.

"I hope so, too. This is my, ah…" he looked to Rosario. He'd been calling her his assistant all this time, but she was so much more than that. She looked at him with a curious smile. "This is my girlfriend Rosario. She's an orca trainer as well and has been alongside me here, as well as in Spain and Portugal at the site of the previous orca attacks." He squeezed her hand. "I'd be lost without her."

Lieutenant Commander Wolf nodded. "I'm well aware. Maybe she can get us un-lost as well."

CHAPTER EIGHTEEN

Jamel's calls and texts were being met with dead silence.

Hadn't he proved to Chet Clarke that he knew what he was talking about?

The latest killer whale assault had been all over the news within the timeframe that Jamel had said it would. Well, at least it had been on the news. Just like Chet, all of the news outlets had gone silent on the matter. It wasn't like there were reporters or bloggers just bobbing around the ocean eager to broadcast what was happening with the freighter.

Just like the various HAARP facilities around the globe, what was happening out there was far from civilization.

He dialed again and got a message that Chet's voicemail was full.

"Come on, man." Jamel flicked the phone onto his desk and twirled in his chair. He stopped himself by poking out his foot until it came in contact with a leg of the desk.

Jumping on his computer, he tapped into a secret satellite feed that tracked energy fluctuations within the ionosphere. The satellite had been launched in 2005, designed to keep a watchful eye on other countries and their own versions of HAARP. Whenever one of them powered up, the satellite could read the supercharging of particles in the ionosphere and backtrack to the source.

He'd noticed the burst of energy coming from Russia's Kalach facility earlier that morning. Over the past several years, he'd learned that it took several hours for the after effects to take place, whether it be a drastic change in temperature, pop up storm or now, scrambling of the brains of killer whales.

Just thinking about it made Jamel feel like the president of the tin foil hat club. No wonder his calls weren't being returned. Offering proof that there would be another killer whale event at a time when they were happening with regularity wasn't enough.

Why killer whales? That one had bothered him for a long time. On the one hand, it made sense because they were the true masters of the world's waterways. No sea beast could stand up to them, especially when they concentrated their efforts. On the other hand, they were also adored by millions. Turning a childhood thrill into an instrument of shock and dread was a page right out of the terrorist playbook.

But there was another reason Jamel suspected they had turned their attention to the killer whales. The mammals had exceedingly acute auditory senses. Part of any HAARP program involved experimentation with audio waves. They were projected on unsuspecting towns and villages to irritate, disorient, fatigue, and yes, control. Now, Jamel had never been privy to any actual lab results on mind control, but it was talked about in hushed tones at the facility. For that alone, he knew it was something they were working on.

Killer whale speech had been studied for decades. Jamel would bet his life some Russian scientist had dedicated his life to finding a way to get inside their heads. It looked like he or she had been successful. And if they could do it to a complex mammal like a killer whale, people were sure to be next.

He'd love to jump on a plane and see Chet face to face, but he had no idea where the man even was at this moment. There was so much to tell him.

A heavy storm rumbled overhead, sheets of rain banging against his windows.

All was quiet on the HAARP front – for now.

He rummaged in the back of his refrigerator for a cold bottle of a double IPA he'd picked up last week. The bitterness felt good as the cold beer passed his lips.

"Time for plan B," he said to his cat, Fort, who was making a rare appearance out from under his bed.

He was always going to enact Plan B, but he'd hoped to have someone with credentials like Chet Clarke on board first.

It looked like that wasn't going to happen now.

The past few hours had been a whirlwind of activity.

Lieutenant Commander Wolf debriefed them on the ride to the Navy base, filling them in on what was really going on. The commercial freighter from Panama had been lost. So far, there were no survivors. News of the tragedy had been suppressed, at least until the military had more answers.

What had been termed a *mega pod* of several hundred orcas had banded together to take down the ship, sacrificing their bodies in order to bring it to a watery grave. Wolf showed them an aerial view of the wreckage. The ship was on its side and sinking fast. Loose cargo intermingled with orca bodies both alive and dead in the cold water.

The pictures made Chet sick to his stomach. Rosario stared at them in cold silence, her green eyes flicking back and forth across the glossy pages. He was almost afraid to ask her what she was thinking.

What really scared him was the fact that what happened to the freighter wasn't the real reason the Navy had come for him.

If things didn't change, the freighter was just going to be the first in a calamitous chain of events.

After an even more intense debriefing at the base with a host of officers in a small conference room, Chet and Rosario were whisked away to a waiting helicopter. Chet was no fan of helicopters, and after their trip, he hoped never to step inside another one again. The green tint to Rosario's face told him she was of the same mind.

They landed aboard the Nimitz class supercarrier somewhere in the Atlantic. The *John Adams* was a nuclear powered aircraft carrier that looked to Chet to be bigger than Delaware and Rhode Island put together. He marveled at how something so unbelievably massive could even stay afloat.

Lieutenant Commander Wolf was to be their escort for their entire trip. He was the first to leave the helicopter, a harsh, cold wind there to greet them. Several men in Navy whites saluted the Lieutenant Commander. They were escorted across the massive deck and taken to the bridge, salutes being snapped off in quick succession.

Rosario gripped Chet's hand the entire time. She'd been very quiet ever since they'd stepped into the black sedan at the hotel. Chet was damn sure she was feeling as overwhelmed as he was.

The bridge looked like something out of a sci-fi movie. Men and women sat at various stations, others purposefully walking about the bridge, all of them, as Chet's father would say, serious as a heart attack.

After watching so many war movies chock full of macho men, it was pleasantly surprising to see so many enlisted women here. It actually made him feel a bit easier. Chet fully appreciated the levelheadedness women brought to the table.

Remembering how Spartan the deck of the Enterprise looked in Star Trek, Chet had to stifle a laugh.

"What would Captain Kirk do with all of this?" he said low and to himself.

To his surprise, Rosario answered, "Find more ways to locate sexy blue aliens to share his bed."

A tall, broad shouldered man with a thick scar bisecting the corner of his upper lip introduced himself as Captain Mitt Stanson. Chet almost saluted until he noticed the man's proffered hand.

"Impressive ship," Chet said, feeling like a school kid on a dream class trip. He'd once taken a tour of a submarine at the Submarine Force Library and Museum in Groton, Connecticut. *Cramped* and *confined* were the two words that came to mind, the smell of grease and age omnipresent in the retired sub.

Not so with the *John Adams*. Everything about it was oversized. The bridge looked like it could accommodate fifty people.

"Thank you," Captain Stanson said. "She's a decent tug." He shook hands with Rosario and even gave a slight bow.

"How close are we to the mega pod?" Lieutenant Commander Wolf asked.

The Captain's jaw clenched. "We should be within shouting distance in an hour."

Chet asked, "Can you tell if any additional whales have joined the mega pod?"

Captain Stanson consulted a tablet. "Yes, from what we can gather, another dozen met up with the mega pod forty minutes ago."

"How many does that make in total?" Rosario said.

Chet tensed, already knowing the ballpark number. Hearing it said out loud, knowing they were in the middle of the ocean heading for the maelstrom, made him queasy.

"We estimate there are about a thousand at this time."

"A thousand," Chet muttered. When they left the base, they'd been told there could be as many as eight hundred. The mega pod was growing at an exponential rate. What could possibly be bringing them all together like this?

Somehow, the Navy thought he'd be the one to tell them. Would they throw him overboard once they realized he was as clueless as everyone else?

"We have extensive video of the mega pod taken from above," Captain Stanson said. "I'll have someone show you to a conference room so you can review it. Maybe there's something you can see there that we're not. It would be good to know how it compares to what you've experienced in Europe and Florida."

"I wished I'd never see something like it again," Chet said. "There are a couple of people I'll need to talk to who were also there in Europe. In fact, I'm waiting on some lab results from an autopsy taken of the orcas in Barcelona."

The Captain nodded. "Not a problem. I'll make sure you get a clear line to them." He checked his watch. "Time's running out until our rendezvous. Let me know if you find anything we can use."

They were summarily dismissed. Lieutenant Commander Wolf asked them to follow him as they made their way to a nearby wood paneled conference room chock full of some top of the line audio-video equipment. No time was wasted. As soon as Chet and Rosario had taken their seats at the round table, bottles of cold water, pads, and pencils were provided by an ensign, the lights were dimmed, and high quality video of the mega pod appeared on a flat screen that ran the length of the opposite wall.

What they saw took their breath away.

To see a thousand imposing orcas rising and falling in the rough water, geysers of mist expelling into the air, creating an unnatural fog around their swelling ranks, was like watching death itself sailing upon the ocean.

"Jesus Christ," Rosario muttered.

Luckily, when the video was taken, there were no other ships in the mega pod's path. Chet couldn't imagine anything surviving such an onslaught.

"This is the same pod that attacked the freighter?" Rosario asked.

Lieutenant Commander Wolf had been standing just to their left with his hands clasped in front of him. "Yes, part of the original pod is there."

"So we know they're not just out for a little exercise," she replied, eyes glued to the screen.

"Not in a pod that big," Chet said. "There's a purpose here. They're hunting."

"But hunting what?" Wolf said.

The back of Chet's scalp prickled. No matter how much he rubbed it, he couldn't get it to stop.

"Anything that gets in their way."

"What happens when *we* get in their way?" Rosario asked.

The lieutenant commander just looked at them, his eyes shifting to his feet.

"They blow them out of the water," Chet said. "Am I right?"

"It would be a last resort," Wolf said.

"And what would be the first?" Rosario said.

"That's what we're hoping you can tell us. Professor Lund promised an answer, but unfortunately, he can no longer provide it."

Chet's gaze snapped away from the mega pod. "Professor Lund? I didn't know you were working with him. Is he on board? I'd like to see him."

Never a big fan of Lund, Chet was aware that the man did have decades more experience watching orcas than he did. His observations could be very useful.

"Professor Lund was here, but there were complications."

"Complications?" Chet said.

Lieutenant Commander Wolf cleared his throat. "He passed away. In fact, his body is still onboard."

"How did it happen?" Rosario asked.

"We believe it was a heart attack. It happened not long after we showed him that video."

"In here?" Chet asked.

All Wolf could do was nod.

Chet's skin wanted to crawl off his bones. For all he knew, he was sitting in the very same seat where Lund had recently died. Rosario got up from her chair, chewing on her thumbnail.

Chet said, "I wonder if seeing a pod as massive as this, knowing that the greatest killing machines in the ocean were gathering in force, scared the life out of him. Lord knows, when they were pummeling that oil rig in Portugal, I had my fair share of heart palpitations. Lund was an old man. He shouldn't have been here."

Wolf was quick to absolve the Navy of any wrongdoing. "He came here voluntarily. In fact, he approached us."

"As opposed to your banging our door down," Rosario added. Her nostrils flared just enough for Chet to realize things were going to get heated if he didn't do something fast. He understood where Rosario was coming from. A man had died and now they were here to do what? Watch the Navy drive a species to extinction?

Chet watched the video of the mega pod. It was impossible to confirm from the vantage point, but he'd bet there were two types of orcas in the mix: resident and offshore orcas. Resident orcas were known to form the largest pods, though nothing like this. Much of the lifestyle of the offshore orca was still a mystery. Offshore orcas were smaller than resident orcas. He saw hundreds of orcas on the smaller side in the video, but without being there, up close, he couldn't tell if they were full grown adults or adolescents. They were named offshore orcas because they were known to travel the greatest distances. It wouldn't be a surprise to learn that a majority of the mega pod was made up of the sub group.

He could only imagine the Tower of Babel going on under those waves with a hundred plus orcas of different dialects talking at once. It boggled the mind that they could function as one unit, considering the mass confusion that should be going on.

"Look, from what I can see, the only thing unusual in their behavior is the fact that they've gathered into such a large pod. That's the problem here. It's like a switch goes off in their heads. In the marine parks, there was no warning, and because they're in such confined quarters with people nearby, fatalities were unfortunately inevitable. Yes, this mega pod is terrifying to look at, but they're in the middle of a vast ocean. From all of the orcas we've observed, whatever sets them into a rampage just as suddenly switches off. In fact, the orca we were working with in Florida exhibited no signs of distress or violence since the attack on her trainer. Once she came out of sedation, it's as if nothing happened."

Wolf took a deep breath, his barrel chest and shoulder rising. "Are you suggesting we tranquilize a thousand killer whales?"

Waving him off, Chet said, "No, that would be impossible. What I am saying is that we need to keep tracking their progression and clear the route they're taking. Warn any ships ahead to get the hell out of there as fast as they can. If we buy enough time, whatever it is that's driving this behavior may just burn itself out."

He felt Rosario's hands on his shoulders.

"Don't engage. Just observe and keep other ships aware," the lieutenant commander said, mulling over Chet's words.

"It's the moral thing to do. We don't know why this is happening, but I can assure you whatever it is, it's outside the control of the orca population. They're somehow being manipulated, but by what, I haven't a clue. That's why I need those lab results from Barcelona tomorrow. Until then, we need to keep both the people and orcas safe."

Rosario gave his shoulders a sharp, painful squeeze. He knew it was a warning not to say anything about Jamel the custodian's HAARP theory. HAARP had been the Navy's pet project, after all. He wasn't sure Wolf would take kindly to being blamed for the outbreak of violence.

"In fact," Chet continued. "It's best we keep our distance from them. They will launch a coordinated attack on this ship the second they see us, no matter how impossible it would be for them to take it down. You can't in good conscience just let them kill themselves in the process. Right now, they're not posing any direct threat. Let's try to keep it that way."

What followed was a deep silence while the video of the mega pod played on. Wolf seemed to be considering Chet's recommendation. Chet didn't know Captain Stanson from a hole in the wall. How he would react to having a civilian basically tell him to stand down was anyone's guess.

One thing he did know was if they willfully engaged the orcas and murdered them, the world would find out. Chet would make sure of it, no matter what the cost.

"Stay right here," Wolf said, his chiseled features softening. "I'll talk to the Captain."

The second the door closed, Chet and Rosario exhaled their held breath.

"Do you think he'll listen?" Rosario said. She still refused to sit. Professor Lund could have died in any one of those seats.

"I may sound delusional, being one guy versus an aircraft carrier full of Navy personnel, but he better."

CHAPTER NINETEEN

"There's a call for you, sir," the voice said outside Chet's cabin.

"I'll be right there," he grumbled, getting out of what passed for a bed. Rosario stirred beside him but didn't wake. She'd been assigned her own cabin, but had snuck in to his in the middle of the night. Neither of them could sleep. He looked at the clock, figuring he'd gotten a cool two hours of z's.

Slipping into yesterday's shirt and pants, he opened the door to find a kid waiting for him. If he was nineteen, Chet would have been surprised.

"I'll take you to the bridge," he said. "It's easy to get turned around here."

"Lead on."

Chet had only seen a small portion of the *John Adams* and could see how one could get easily lost. Oddly enough, the floating behemoth reminded him of the Mall of America in Minneapolis. He'd visited there once, walking around for five hours. The multilevel mall was jammed with more stores and restaurants than most metropolitan cities. It even had an amusement park and aquarium *inside*! When he'd told a local what he'd seen, she'd said, "Oh honey, you only saw like twenty percent of the mall. You need a few days to really take it all in."

Captain Stanson was there to greet him on the bridge. Unlike Chet, he looked like he'd gotten a peaceful night's sleep, if that was even possible when you were in charge of something as massive and impressive as the *John Adams*.

Chet's estimation of the man was perhaps larger than the supercarrier because he'd pulled back and out of the way of the mega pod. They kept tabs on their progression by constant air surveillance. Before Chet retired that night, the mega pod had grown to over twelve-hundred orcas. That meant whatever was driving them was still strong as ever. Chet prayed that they had splintered off overnight.

"How's the mega pod?" he asked.

"Living up to its name, I'm afraid."

"Damn."

"I have a call from Raquel Suarez and Ivan Padron for you," the Captain said, offering him a cup of coffee that he couldn't say no to. He handed Chet a headset, wheeling over a plush chair and giving him some space.

"Ivan, Raquel, I hope you have something good to tell me." He burned his lips and tongue on the coffee. It was so strong, he felt like he'd been goosed.

"Fuck hope," Ivan growled. "We have nothing."

"Nothing? How is that possible?"

Raquel spoke up. "Every single test is negative. There's no sign of any foreign antibody or contamination."

Chet stared out the row of windows at the vast, endless expanse of blue sky and bluer sea. This was not a good way to start the day.

"That's impossible."

"That's what I said," Ivan said in the background. Chet pictured him pacing around the room, looking like a lunatic. "We're asking the lab to run every damn test again. If they screwed up the first time, I'll have their balls."

"Most of them are women," Raquel added, dryly.

"No difference. I know plenty of women with more balls than most men."

Chet sat straighter in his chair. The tension building in his lower back threatened to lock him into a hunch. "What about the brain?"

"Normal," Raquel said.

"Not even a single thing out of the ordinary?"

"I wish I could say yes."

He noticed Captain Stanson throwing concerned glances his way. Chet moved the attached microphone closer to his mouth and spoke lower. "Would concentrated radio waves have a lasting impact...shit, any impact on an orca brain?"

Ivan and Raquel were silent for longer than Chet wanted.

"What the hell are you talking about?" Ivan said.

"I'm not entirely sure. Raquel, you've seen more orca brains than me. Would there be a visible difference in a brain subjected to massive radio waves?"

She sighed. "No one knows that answer because it's never been studied. Why do you keep talking about radio waves?"

He gripped the coffee cup so hard, a dribble of scalding coffee blistered his hand. He was too preoccupied to care. "It's just a theory. If you were here, I could go into it in more detail."

"Then tell your captain to get us there," Ivan said.

"I'm not sure that would even be possible. We're deep in the Atlantic, following a pod of orcas twelve-hundred strong and growing."

"Twelve-hundred!" Raquel exclaimed. That was followed by a very obvious call to God, Jesus and the Virgin Mary in Spanish.

"Where are they going?" Ivan asked, sounding closer to the phone. He was probably leaning over Raquel, breathing coffee breath in her face.

"We don't know. The Navy is keeping tabs on what they're calling a mega pod while also keeping their distance. All ships have been warned to stay the hell away."

"Orcas are fast. They can change direction in seconds and you'd never catch up to them or be able to warn people in time."

Chet's empty stomach gurgled, a bubble of acid tingling his throat. He either needed food or a Valium.

He said, "So far, the mega pod is maintaining a pretty straight line, sticking to a latitude of twenty-five degrees north. That would put them on a trajectory towards Western Sahara."

"Why would they go there?" Ivan asked.

"For the shopping, of course," Chet said, exasperated. "I don't think they give a shit what body of land stands in their way. I just keep hoping whatever is making them gather like this will stop before they even get close to land…and civilization."

"Get us on that ship," Ivan said again.

Chet jumped when a hand touched his shoulder. "Where are they?" Captain Stanson asked.

"Huh?"

"Ivan and Raquel. I understand they've been working on this since the start of the outbreak."

"You were listening to me?"

"This is my ship, and everything that happens onboard is my business." He didn't say it as a threat, just as a matter of fact. As much as Chet wanted to be mad, he had assumed his conversation was being listened to, which is why he didn't go into detail about the whole radio wave theory. After coming up snake eyes on the lab tests, he didn't have much else to cling to. "So, where do we need to go to pick them up?"

Chet locked eyes with the captain and said to Ivan and Raquel, "You guys might want to pack a bag."

Chet was reviewing the latest film when Rosario burst into the room.

"The mega pod stopped!"

He slowly rose from his chair, pausing the video.

"What do you mean, stopped?"

Rosario's hair was pulled back and tied with a black band. She'd complained earlier that she'd forgotten to bring any makeup, but she looked stunning to him. He was sure most of the crew would agree.

"I just ran into Wolf. He'd been on the bridge when the call came in that the pod is in some kind of holding pattern. They haven't made any forward progress in the past ten minutes."

"Have they broken up?"

He knew that once the mega pod splintered off into dozens and dozens of groups, whatever it was that was herding them together had lost its hold. The hope was that it happened before the mega pod came in contact with any ships.

Rosario shook her head. "Not yet. But the Captain is sending more jets to do some flybys."

Tapping a pencil on the conference table, Chet wondered aloud. "What made them stop? And why?"

"Maybe they're just resting."

"Normally, I'd say over a thousand orcas taking a siesta at the same time was completely insane, but I'm not so sure. We'll need to see the latest video to be sure."

She held her hand out to him. "And that's why I'm here. We've been summoned to the bridge so we can watch it live."

They hustled to the bridge, only getting turned around once. Lieutenant Commander Wolf stood next to Captain Stanson. Both men were staring at a monitor above them.

"That's a live feed?" Chet asked.

"As live as it can get," Wolf said.

The image was surprisingly clear and steady. Chet assumed it was being taken by a helicopter.

Seeing a thousand orcas in motion was terrifying. Watching them congregate in an enormous circle, packed together tightly, was enough to dry up all of the saliva in his mouth.

"Any chance they can get closer or zoom in?" he asked.

Captain Stanson told the crewman sitting beside him to order the surveillance team to get a tighter shot.

Seconds later, he had a clear view of a section of the mega pod. The orcas were moving about lazily, rising and clearing their blowholes so they could breath.

"A little closer," he said, hands gripping the back of an empty chair.

"I was right," Rosario said.

"Looks like I'm rubbing off on you," he replied.

He didn't bother to face the look he knew she was giving him.

About a hundred orcas of every size imaginable filled the screen. He'd been right, too. These were resident orcas mixed with offshore orcas.

"Just wild," he whispered.

"What do you make of it?" Captain Stanson said, pulling Chet's attention away from the monitor.

"They're sleeping."

"All of them?"

"Can you ask them to pull back now? I want to see the perimeter of the mega pod."

When the view changed, Chet jabbed the screen with the pad of his index finger.

"See that?"

Chet guessed about a hundred orcas milled about the sleeping mega pod.

"What am I seeing?" the Captain asked.

"They have sentries watching out for the pod. See how it looks like they're patrolling the edges?"

While orcas had to be in constant motion in order to stay alive, there were degrees of movement that told an experienced marine biologist which ones were asleep and which ones were not. The sentry orcas moved faster, covering their seemingly assigned territory over and over again. They were all adult orcas. Guarding the mega pod was too important a task to leave to the young. Chet wasn't surprised. Orcas were exceedingly intelligent. Having the wherewithal to post sentries was more chilling than shocking.

Lieutenant Commander Wolf narrowed his gaze at the monitor. "Now would be an optimal time to see if we can get them to disperse."

"How do you plan on doing that?" Rosario asked.

"We could drop a small explosive right in the middle of the mega pod," Captain Stanson replied, sounding as if this wasn't something he'd just come up with.

"You can't do that!" Chet said, holding himself back from grabbing the Captain's arm. That wouldn't go over well at all.

The Captain said, "I can, but for the moment, I choose not to. I only hope I don't live to regret my decision."

"Sir, they're going to descend to get as close as possible," the crewman said, one hand on the headset.

"Tell them to proceed. Might be the best chance we get." The Captain turned to Chet and Rosario. "You ready for a gift?"

"A gift?" Chet said.

"We've made plans to tranquilize one of the smaller killer whales and bring it back to the ship so you can study it."

"You can do that?"

Captain Stanson flashed a rigid smile. "We're the US Navy. We can do anything we set our minds to."

"How are you going to get it out of the mega pod?"

"With heavy duty cargo nets. Because of weight limitations, we're going to have to select the smallest we can find, but that should be enough, I assume?"

Chet's brain fired off so many possibilities, both good and bad, that could come about from trying to study an orca still in the throes of whatever this was that controlled them. He could only nod.

Rosario pinched his back, whispering in his ear, "You can't be serious."

"Maybe if we separate it from the mega pod, it will revert to its normal self."

"And maybe it will lash out and kill us or anyone helping us."

"That won't be an issue," Wolf said.

"Why is that?" Rosario asked.

"The killer whale will be euthanized the moment we detect any trouble."

"So you're bringing one of their babies here just to kill it?" Chet felt a wave of heat coming off Rosario. He was transfixed by the image on the monitor. The helicopter was getting so close, the rotor wash was kicking up the water, hundreds of tiny white caps dancing around the slumbering orcas. The exhalation from their blowholes was hammered by the wind, rapidly raining back down on them.

"We're hoping it won't come to that," Captain Stanson said. "I think this is the lesser of two evils. Don't you agree?"

"No, I don't," she said.

Wolf interjected. "Look, we can't just sit idly by and watch forever. If the mega pod doesn't break up before they come close to land, action will have to be taken."

Before Rosario could object, Chet grabbed her hand. "Do you see that?"

The orcas were so close together, it looked like he could walk along their backs and never touch water. Their sleek bodies rubbed against one another as they dove and rose.

It was beautiful.

So many wonderful animals coexisting with one another, taking comfort in their close proximity. Maybe he was making more of it than it actually was, but that didn't make it any less breathtaking.

Right in the center of a swarm of bodies was a baby orca, maybe no more than a year old. It was sandwiched between two adults. Getting it out from between them would be no easy task.

With so little room to maneuver, how would they get it in the cargo net?

"And once they separate it from its mother and manage not to murder it, what are we supposed to do? Take it home with us and care for it?" Rosario said.

"I guess we'd have to make arrangements to bring it to one of the marine parks," he said, feeling like a traitor as soon as he heard his own words.

"That's exactly what we want to stop," she not so gently reminded him.

He didn't know how to answer that wouldn't make him sound like a hypocrite and piss her off even more.

Chet had never felt so out of his depth. What the hell was he doing on a Navy supercarrier observing a mega pod of orcas? How did they expect him to know what the hell to do? If he could have one wish at the moment, it would be to bring Professor Lund back from the dead so all of the focus wasn't on him.

The Navy had marine biologists, but the two that were onboard had deferred to him. They were there solely in the capacity to assist Chet when needed. Both men, whom he'd met briefly the night before, were about as green as stalks of broccoli. Chet had seen and worked with more orcas in a month than they had in their lives.

Rosario whirled and stormed off the bridge. Wolf and Stanson didn't even notice her go. All of their attention was on the monitor. Chet looked back and thought of going after her.

"Tell him to proceed with the tranquilizer," Captain Stanson said.

No, he realized he needed to be here to witness this. There was nothing he could do to stop it anyway. It was best to observe it from start to finish and if he was lucky, be part of the solution, preferably one that didn't include mass slaughter.

The helicopter was so close, Chet was able to see the small dart bury itself in the back of the baby orca.

It reacted violently, thrashing about. There was no sound on the monitor, but Chet could very well imagine the wails the orca was making.

"Is that normal?" the Captain asked.

Chet said, "No, not at all. It should have barely felt the dart. It's acting as if your man dropped a long harpoon into it."

The baby orca's wild reaction appeared to wake the adult orcas around it. In seconds, the ocean was frothing with orca activity.

"Something's wrong," Chet said. "Your men should pull back."

"There's finally some separation," Captain Stanson said. "Get it in the net, now!"

His orders were relayed to the men in the chopper.

Chet watched a line come into the frame, a giant black net unfurling from its end. It landed beside the baby orca.

The picture enlarged as the chopper got even closer.

Chet had to remind himself to breathe. All eyes on the bridge were locked on the monitor.

In an instant, all of the adult orcas around the baby dove deep and out of sight, leaving it on its own.

"It's like they're giving it to us," Wolf said, his voice uneven.

"I don't think they are," Chet said.

A second later, he was proved right.

CHAPTER TWENTY

Five adult orcas burst from the ocean, heading straight for the helicopter.

Chet watched in horror as one of them locked its jaws on the landing skid. The picture canted hard to the left as the weight of the orca dragged the chopper down with startling speed into the cold water.

The video cut out instantly.

Everyone on the bridge was frozen in stunned silence.

Finally, Captain Stanson turned to Chet and said, "Why didn't you tell me that could happen?"

Chet's blood rushed to his face. "What makes you think I knew they were going to attack the helicopter?"

The Captain's posture and demeanor were so preternaturally calm, it worried Chet far more than if he were screaming and losing his shit.

"I just lost five good men."

Lieutenant Commander Wolf looked to Chet with a mix of pity and anger. How the hell had this become his fault?

"There was no way I could have predicted that," he said in his defense. "I had no idea how close the helicopter was hovering over them. Orcas do breach the water, but I've never seen any go that high."

One of the crewmen interjected, "Sir, it appears the mega pod is on the move again."

"Have they broken up at all?"

They waited for a tense moment.

"No, sir."

"Then it looks like we're going to have to help them along."

"Please, don't do that," Chet said. The return glare from the Captain made him mute.

There was no way of defending the orcas now. They may have been intelligent, but they couldn't know their action was a declaration of war.

Another monitor came to life, showing a fast moving image of the ocean. There were crosshairs in the center of the screen and a ton of changing readouts on the periphery.

When Chet was a boy, he remembered watching the bombing runs on Iraq in the first gulf war. It had been like watching a video game, only the explosions were real. For him, there had always been a disconnect. It looked so small on their TV screen, he thought he could see the flaws in the graphic designer's programming.

There was no disconnect this time.

Forcing himself not to turn away, he watched as a jet screamed over the mega pod. Something narrow and fast tore toward the center of the mega pod.

A great geyser of water and shattered orca bodies exploded high into the air.

Chet was grateful Rosario wasn't here to see it.

"Direct hit," the crewman said without a hint of emotion.

"Now let's see how these sons of bitches react," Wolf said under his breath.

"The orcas aren't our enemy," Chet reminded him.

"Right now, they're certainly not our friends," the lieutenant commander shot back.

The families of the men in the chopper and trainers at the marine parks in the US and Spain would agree with the man.

"The mega pod is dispersing."

A restrained cheer went up from the crew. The Captain remained stoic.

Sick to his stomach that it had come to murdering the orcas, Chet felt a glimmer of hope that the explosion had somehow shaken them from their collective fugue.

"I want more eyes in the sky tracking each pod," Captain Stanson said. "If they look like they're going to regroup, we'll hit them again."

"How fast can they go?" Lieutenant Commander Wolf asked Chet.

"Up to thirty-five miles an hour, sometimes faster for short bursts."

"Thank you. We'll call you if and when we need you. Until then, it's best to wait in the conference room and we'll send current video for you to review."

Just like that, Chet was dismissed.

He stormed off the bridge just as Rosario had done earlier.

They were not asked to return to the bridge. Rosario cried when Chet told her what had been done. He'd taken a few blows to his chest. She didn't blame him. He was just convenient to vent her frustration.

They stayed in the conference room for hours, drinking coffee. Chet had made a list of possible reasons for the violent and strange orca behavior. No theory was too crazy. He even jotted down 'virus from Mars' on one line.

He and Rosario worked down the list, poking holes in each theory.

"I seriously don't think it's physical," Rosario said. She'd taken to pacing over the past hour, pausing every now and then to twirl a chair around and around until Chet got dizzy just looking at it. "If it was, Raquel's tests would have showed something."

"Not necessarily true," Chet said. "I don't know squat about the lab she uses and their track record. There could be contamination."

"For the orcas in Spain *and* Portugal?"

"Stranger things have happened."

She blew stray hairs from her eyes. "Stranger things *are* happening. How long until you get any results from Naala's bloodwork?"

"Another couple of days. That's too long for me."

"Not if this keeps up."

Chet stared at the closed door. Every now and then, they heard people hustling past. He kept waiting for Wolf to make an appearance. The military man was either pissed at them or whatever was currently going on with the fractured mega pod was commanding his full attention.

Rosario leaned against the whiteboard, tenting her fingers under her dimpled chin. "So let's just say it's not physical. Which leads us to it being mental."

"The collective orca subconscious losing it at the same time across the globe?" he said, trying hard to hide his sarcasm.

"I take it you weren't a fan of Jung in school."

"I think I drank all the Jung lessons out of my head in college."

She went back to pacing. "Jesus, I hate to say it, but what if this is some kind of mind control. Could that HAARP stuff really be capable of all this?"

HAARP was listed on the legal pad with a question mark next to it, along with Jamel Abrams. Double question mark.

He tossed the pad on the table. "I could sooner tell you about Katy Perry's personal life than I can HAARP. I thought we were going to let this one go, seeing as a janitor being the only one holding the keys to the truth seems pretty damn unlikely."

"Custodian," she corrected him.

"Right. Besides, weren't you the one who dismissed that guy outright?" He twirled a pencil, admiring the sly smile on Rosario's lips.

"I was. A woman has a right to change her mind."

Chet snapped the pencil between his fingers when the door swung open.

"Get off your lazy asses. We have work to do."

"Ivan!" Chet exclaimed. After the mega pod had broken up, Chet assumed they had cancelled the order to bring Ivan and Raquel to the supercarrier.

The Spaniard looked disheveled but determined.

"They flew me here on a jet that went faster than your president's mouth."

Chet rose from his chair and took his hand. Ivan gave Rosario a quick hug and a peck on each cheek.

"What about Raquel?" Rosario asked.

"They already have her working on the orcas."

"What orcas?" Chest said.

"They retrieved five bodies. Come on, she needs all the help she can get. Those marine biologists don't know their assholes from a knothole."

They were escorted to the deck, the walk feeling like a good mile from the conference room. A makeshift autopsy lab had been constructed with a heavy gray tarp rigged over both bodies and work area.

"Looks like the boys in white have been busy," Rosario remarked.

Raquel raised an eyebrow when they entered. She was covered in gore from shoulders to feet.

"I only have one whole orca. The rest is just bits and pieces," she said in way of a greeting. Ivan passed a box of latex gloves around and they got busy.

They worked at a feverish pace, but managed to be careful as well. The last thing they wanted to do was botch the labs because of shoddy work.

It was exhausting, cutting through the layers of fat, sawing through bone and lifting hunks of flesh so heavy, Chet was certain he'd aggravated his old hernia. Ivan cataloged and labeled while Rosario took copious notes, both on a pad and through the voice recorder on her phone.

When they were done two hours later, Raquel threw her gloves on the deck and said, "Where the hell is the shower?" Her face was beaded with sweat.

"You'll have time for that later," Lieutenant Commander Wolf said, stepping under the tarp. "For now, I need you all to come with me."

Ivan looked like he was about to tell Wolf to do something physically impossible to himself. Chet motioned for him to keep calm. Out here in the middle of the Atlantic, the Navy was fully in charge.

They followed Wolf in a single file line, the two Navy marine biologists staying behind to clean things up.

It had been sunny and a tad warm when they'd entered the tarp. Now, the sky was pink and the air cool. Chet thought he smelled rain in the air, but there wasn't a cloud to be seen.

Wolf took them to a much less appointed conference room. It had a rectangular table and several serviceable chairs that were obviously not built for comfort. The walls were bare and the room had a slight echo.

Captain Stanson was seated, waiting for them.

"Is this the brig?" Chet asked, half-joking.

"If it was, you'd know it," the Captain said, gesturing for them to take a seat. Chet could only imagine how bad they smelled. The man didn't seem to notice…or if he did, he didn't care.

"Any preliminary findings?" he asked the group.

"Not a fucking thing, other than severe damage from your weapons," Ivan replied, sitting straight in his chair, eyes boring into the Captain. Chet had told him about the Navy's bombing of the mega pod. Even though Ivan had lost very good people to the orcas in his care, the last thing he wanted was to see them slaughtered.

Captain Stanson turned to Raquel.

"From what I can tell, everything appears normal," she said, hands folded in front of her. "We'll look at the blood and tissue, but I'm afraid we'll come up with more of the same."

"That's not what I was hoping to hear." He drummed his fingers on a closed file folder.

"That makes all of us," Chet said.

"So what you're telling me is that, in your professional opinions, there's nothing that can be done?"

Chet cleared his throat, tamping down the anger he felt bubbling up. "Right now, as far as finding causality for their behavior, we're stumped. That's not to say that the answer isn't waiting for us in the lab. But truth be told, orcas are wild animals. Even if we do find the root cause of their unexplained…madness, I'm not sure what we can do other than steer clear of them."

"Or kill them," Rosario said, glaring at the Captain.

"We may be the apex predators on land, but they hold the title on the sea," Chet continued. "As much as we like to think we're in charge of this planet, we can't control everything."

Lieutenant Commander Wolf visibly bristled. "So we're just supposed to allow them to disrupt all of our commercial, private and military operations? Do you know what that would do to our economy? Or our ability to properly defend our country?"

"I'm well aware of that," Chet said, palms flat on the table in a conscious effort not to ball them into fists.

"So we just sit and play the role of spectators," Wolf said with a derisive snort.

Now Chet flew from his chair. "I don't know what you're trying to get me to say! I feel just as helpless as you do. I've dedicated my life to protecting and caring for them. Jesus, I despise the fact that we keep them penned in marine parks, which is why I made it a point to be there, making sure they're treated properly."

He cast a quick glance at Ivan who caught his eye and looked away.

"It kills me to see what they've done. And I'm sick to my soul knowing that the only way people are going to feel safe is if the threat is eliminated. At least the orcas can't control what they're doing." Chet felt a tremor run through his body. Saying all of his fears aloud wasn't cathartic.

It just made him feel all the more helpless.

The Captain opened the folder. "Who is Jamel Abrams?"

"Come again?" Chet said, his heart starting to gallop.

He was shown the legal pad he and Rosario were working on. "I'm very interested to know why you wrote HAARP down as a possible reason for our current situation and who this Jamel Abrams might be."

Rosario's hand found Chet's under the table.

"It's time we were completely open and honest with one another," Captain Stanson said, leaning forward in his chair. "Because we now have four pods of three hundred killer whales each heading in different directions at breakneck speed. Before more people...and killer whales...die, we need to come clean."

CHAPTER TWENTY-ONE

Chet was never so nervous in his life. He felt like a world class lunatic recounting everything Jamel Abrams had told him about HAARP and the Russian's experimentation with mind control. Ivan and Raquel listened to him without saying a word. He was pretty sure they didn't even blink, such was their shock.

The Captain and Lieutenant Commander asked him questions when he started to sputter, unsure if he should go on. They prodded him like interrogation experts, letting up only when it was apparent he had nothing left to say.

Through it all, Rosario kept her hand firmly planted on his knee, pressing it reassuringly as he babbled on.

Captain Stanson had been taking notes the entire time.

When Chet was done, he slumped back in his chair, exhausted and embarrassed.

"You say the Russian installation is in Karach, correct?" the Captain asked, looking down at his notes.

Chet waved him off. "No, I don't say it. Jamel Abrams said it."

"Right. And again, how did he come about this information?"

"I told you, he said he worked at the HAARP facility in Alaska."

"As a janitor," Wolf said.

Chet deflated even more, if that was possible. "Yes. If he's the same Jamel Abrams from Connecticut, he's also possibly a scientist."

"Who decided to become a janitor," Wolf said.

"Exactly."

"He could have been messed up," Ivan said. "Drugs, breakdown, divorce. I've seen worse things happen to smarter people."

Rosario sat up straighter in her chair. "Or he could have used his job as a janitor to sneak around. He's a conspiracy guy. Maybe he thought the only way to get the truth was to be given the kind of access to the facility that only a janitor would have. Don't secret bases have a whole need to know policy? That would mean the left hand wouldn't always know what the right was up to. You keep them within their tracks with blinders on. But a janitor, who cares where he goes or what he sees? Brilliant people can be elitist, which can lead to major blind spots. A janitor is obviously too stupid to even have a simple grasp of what's going on around him. Give him the keys to the whole place because garbage cans need to be emptied, floors mopped and toilets cleaned. It's not like the chimp with a push broom will be able to put two and two together."

"Unless that chimp is a scientist in his own right," Chet muttered.

"Do you have his number?" Captain Stanson asked, seemingly hooked by Rosario's theory. Chet was as well. It was the only one that made sense. Not that much of what had happened over the past week made much sense.

"Yes." Chet took out his phone and scrolled through the log. When he found Jamel's last call, he showed the man the number, which he then wrote down. At this moment, Chet wished he'd called Jamel and heard him out more. Little did he know, the man's theory, wild as it was, might be the closest to the truth.

The Captain consulted his own phone.

"That's an Alaska area code," he said.

"So this is why you were asking me if concentrated radio waves could affect an orca brain," Raquel spoke up for the first time since Chet had spilled the conspiracy beans.

"Look, I was grasping at straws."

"We didn't want to believe it, but we have to explore every possibility," Rosario added.

The Captain consulted Chet's notes. "Including a virus from Mars?"

"Look, we're not crazy," Chet said.

Only crazy people insist they're not crazy, he thought.

"You guys invented HAARP," Chet said. "You should know its capabilities more than anyone. Why ask me about it when I only got the information secondhand?"

"I assure you, HAARP was not developed for mind control," the Captain said, eyes down at his notes.

"Yours and the Soviet's governments also denied remote viewing for decades, but now we know you were lying through your teeth," Ivan said, coming to Chet's rescue. "You poisoned prisoners with LSD in the fifties and sixties in mind control experiments. So forgive us if we're not falling all over ourselves to believe you this time."

Wolf pounded his fist on the table. "What would be the goddamn point in scrambling the brains of a bunch of killer whales?"

"You said it yourself," Chet said. "Disrupt the economy and military of nations around the world. This could just be the first step."

An overhead speaker squawked. "Requesting the Captain report to the bridge."

Captain Stanson closed the file and stood. "I told them to interrupt me for one thing only. Ladies and gentlemen, if you will please follow me. I believe we have another cluster fuck on our hands."

He wasn't exaggerating.

A bank of monitors showed the four splintered pods from above. Hundreds of orcas were cleaving through the ocean, heading to all four points of the compass. Even though each pod was a quarter the size of the mega pod, they were no less awe inspiring and terrifying to watch.

Next to each image was a graphic on a map showing the estimated location each pod was heading for. If they stayed on course, ports in Morocco, Turks and Caicos, Brazil and Iceland were in the line of fire.

Of course, the Atlantic Ocean was vast and the orcas were fast and versatile. They could change course at any time. It was really all guesswork on the part of the Navy.

"That's not all," the Captain said, handing his tablet over to Chet. Rosario, Ivan and Raquel peered at it over his shoulder.

"My God," Chet mumbled.

There were reports from every marine park around the globe of orcas attacking trainers. At one park in China, their orca had leapt over the safety glass during a show, crushing a dozen school children in the front row on a class trip.

Chet opened each report, scanning it quickly then moving on to the next.

After the curated list of marine park attacks, there was news of pods gathering in the Pacific Ocean. Orcas everywhere had gone collectively murderous.

A new video was fed into the monitors, this time showing the mega pod they'd been following. The mega pod had circled their wagons around a family of humpback whales. The giant humpbacks were no match for the crazed orcas. Instead of their usual hunting methods, they simply attacked at once, shredding the defenseless whales in minutes. The water boiled crimson as each orca snatched away their pound of flesh and blubber.

"Jesus Christ," someone muttered.

"They have to eat," Chet said, horrified by the sheer brutality but understanding the necessity. "They're burning a lot of calories with this trek across the Atlantic. It's only going to get worse. With their numbers now, nothing poses a challenge to them."

"Wait," Rosario said, taking the tablet from Chet's sweaty grasp. She walked away from the group, staring at the screen.

"This all happened in the last hour," Captain Stanson said. "Every military is now on high alert. You understand how we can no longer sit back and wait for whatever it is that's affecting them to wear itself out."

Chet rubbed his eyes with the heel of his hands until his eyes hurt.

What hurt even more was that he did understand the Captain.

"So what are you going to do?" Ivan said.

"Blow them out of the fucking water," Lieutenant Commander Wolf growled.

Captain Stanson gave him a sharp look, as if to tell the man to stand down. Wolf retreated to another section of the busy bridge.

"You can't," Raquel said.

"We have to," the Captain replied, his attention drawn to someone who was handing him another tablet.

"He's right," Rosario said. She walked back toward them, gripping the tablet.

"There has to be another fucking way," Ivan said without much conviction.

Rosario shook her head. "No, not the Captain. Jamel Abrams. He's right. Here, see for yourself."

Taking the tablet back, Chet scrolled through the long list of reports and the links to images and video.

"I don't see anything," he said.

Rosario beamed. "Exactly!" Her exclamation was loud enough to garner the attention of everyone within earshot. "What don't you see? Russia! They have a few marine parks. There's not a single report of a disturbance there. Also, if you look, none of the herding orcas are anywhere near Russian waters."

That got Captain Stanson's attention. He held out his hand for Chet to pass him the tablet.

Chet was slightly buoyed by the news, but he had to play Devil's advocate. "That may be the case, but the Russians aren't the best at telling the world when things shit the bed."

"That may have been the case in the past, but not so anymore," the Captain said. "Even Russia can't hide the truth anymore. This is going to have to be kicked up the chain of command."

Chet pulled Rosario close. "You may have just saved thousands of orcas."

"I'm afraid to say anything and jinx it."

"We have another problem," the Captain said. "One that we may need all of you to attend to."

Jamel Abrams saw the news and realized he'd have to enact his plan B sooner than expected.

The killer whales had gone collectively insane. At the current count, over thirty-five people had lost their lives in various water park attacks. Another hundred and counting had occurred in open water as the killer whales assaulted anything in their way of congregating to form enormous and fast traveling pods.

He checked his HAARP observation program and saw the high amount of energy being pushed out of Kalach in Russia. He wasn't sure how they were doing this, affecting such a wide swath of the killer whale population, but there was no doubt in his mind they were behind everything.

Chet Clarke had gone dark on him. Jamel wondered if he had gotten too close to the fray and was now resting in the belly of a killer whale.

He had to talk to someone. He dialed up Sam on the east coast.

There was no answer.

Damn.

He went to the fridge and popped open another IPA. Ever since things had started going sideways, the bottles of local beer had been going down his throat with alarming frequency.

"You can't get blackout drunk," he warned himself, taking as small a sip as possible.

Sitting back in his small command center, he scanned the small open windows of various live news reports, each one focusing on a specific and fresh killer whale attack.

The world was in a panic, and rightfully so.

If they knew what was behind everything, perhaps it would lessen their fear. Knowledge was power. Power against the darkness and anxiety.

Lord knows, Jamel had gleaned more than his fair share of knowledge over the years. Graduating high school at fifteen, he had a wide open future before him with endless possibilities. He'd breezed through Caltech, private companies courting him in his junior year for prominent positions within their science divisions. For a time, he was sure he'd end up in bioengineering.

Then he'd heard about HAARP, and the more he learned, the more intrigued he became. His obsessive leanings that had helped him tackle his studies with a burning fervor found a new, shiny object, and they wouldn't let him walk away. Using some vital contacts in the scientific community, he'd met with several former employees, and what he'd learned changed his life forever.

He supposed the deeper down the rabbit hole he went, he may have had a slight mental break. It had always been the concern of his mother, a maid for a local motel back home. She'd often said the line between genius and madness was thinner than a mouse's ass crack.

It didn't matter now. Genius or insane, he did know the truth. His time spent undercover at the HAARP facility had confirmed all of his worst fears. He'd had unfettered access to the entire facility, and he spent his time wisely, connecting the dots from snatches of conversations, scraps of paper and glimpses at the endless array of monitors. To a lay person, it would have all just been a hodgepodge of science gobbled-gook. Jamel was not a lay person, though he often envied those who were.

During his two year stint at HAARP, he'd gathered enough intelligence to blow the lid off the whole thing, but the big question was always, who would believe him? That doubt forced him to take risks, to linger too long in labs and strain too hard to listen in whenever several scientists gathered. He noticed they had started to give him the side-eye, this custodian who always seemed to be around, lingering.

Feeling as if they were getting wise to his con, he'd quit, signing reams of NDAs and telling his boss he needed to go home to take care of his ailing mother.

Mom was fine, though he supposed worried every day about her son who could have been anything he wanted and ended up a recluse in Alaska.

Taking a deep breath, he opened up the press release he'd written days ago. It needed a few more passes, and he had to incorporate the latest developments. Once he felt it was ready, and there really wasn't much time anymore, he'd send it to every single news agency in the world. If he had blown the whistle even weeks earlier, he would have been summarily discredited and dismissed. Now, by tying in the facts with the brutal news that was plastered on every screen, there was a chance they'd listen.

A tiny alarm pulled him away from the document to check his HAARP monitor.

"Uh-oh."

The HAARP array in his own backyard was not only online again. It was going full bore, but at what he couldn't be sure.

He gave a quick fist bump.

Maybe Chet Clarke had listened to him and gotten the ear of someone higher up.

"Fight fire with mother fucking fire," he said, watching the readout climb up and up as more ELF waves were rocketed into the ionosphere.

CHAPTER TWENTY-TWO

A series of interconnecting flights brought Chet, Rosario, Ivan and Raquel to an island facility off the western coast of Ireland. To say their lives had been in a whirlwind over the past twenty-four hours was like saying China had a fair number of people living within its borders.

The sun had burned off the morning haze. Only a handful of white clouds were visible on the horizon. The serenity above was in stark contrast to the tempest below.

They stepped off another helicopter, Chet's stomach in knots, onto the roof of a squat, square building. Unlike on the supercarrier *John Adams*, there was no one there to greet them. The helicopter powered down, the pilot staying inside.

A second helicopter landed on the other end of the roof.

They had been too late.

Not exactly. The unforeseen had made itself…seen.

A pod of orcas that had not been on their radar had seemingly appeared out of nowhere, descending on the island lab like locusts. The waters around the small island were alive, tossed into whitecaps and foam from the unimaginable battle taking place under and above the surface.

"Where did everyone go?" Ivan said.

Chet looked over the edge of the rooftop. They were surrounded by chaos. Orca bodies, hundreds of them, squirmed and dove, leapt and cried out. He flinched when he saw an adult orca pinwheel into the air. It had not done so of its own volition.

"Looks like they evacuated. From what Captain Stanson told me, they were nothing but glorified babysitters. Funding for this project was minimal."

Raquel sneered as she watched the battle below. "What did they think they were possibly going to do with them?"

"Study them," Chet said. "At least until the money ran out."

"So why hide them?" Rosario asked.

"Because they scare the hell out of people. No one wants to know some of these things survived."

These things were the remnants of the prehistoric chimera fish, or better known to the public as ghost sharks, that had impossibly sprung from a chasm in the Atlantic several years earlier. They had stormed the coast of Miami, ending in an all out sea battle that ended, at least as far as the world was concerned, in the utter extinction of the chimera fish for the second time in their history.

The chimera fish were as ugly as they were fierce, their mottled flesh so corpse-like, wide mouths armed with jaws capable of crushing steel. They looked utterly alien, and in a sense, they were. The holdouts from man's prehistoric past were a sight to behold.

Chet had known Brad Whitely, the marine biologist who had spearheaded the mission to find the origin point of the enormous fish and eradicate them. Killing them was an easy decision to make. Some of the chimera fish were over fifty feet long. All of them were killing machines the likes of which the modern world had never seen. After millions of years trapped in ice, they came back from the dead ravenous and powerful.

Whitely had disappeared from the public eye weeks after the fish had been hunted down and destroyed. Dead chimera fish were on display in museums all over the world. As far as Chet was concerned, that was that. The crisis had lasted a little over a week, but it was over.

It appeared he'd been wrong.

A band of chimera fish had been accidentally discovered by an oil drilling team, months after the Miami skirmish. Only this time, they had been captured, corralled and kept well fed to avoid another outbreak.

Captain Stanson advised them that there were ten chimera fish in total, the smallest at twenty-four feet, the largest topping out just under sixty feet in length. Only the United Kingdom and United States governments knew of the existence of the holding facility. They'd found out early that testing the fish was difficult and dangerous. They were almost impossible to sedate. They responded to only one thing – food.

When the Captain saw one of the pods headed north toward Iceland, he worried that it could shift course and end up on the outskirts of Ireland. That pod was still going strong toward Iceland.

This new pod was the one that had unwittingly let the chimera fish out of the bag, so to speak.

They had been flown here to find a way to divert the orcas. Blocking the ELF waves from Russia's HAARP was out of the question. Chet learned that the Earth itself was an antenna for ELF waves. There was literally no way to stop them.

Which meant they had to draw the orcas away from the lab housing the chimera fish. His idea was to program a series of decoded orca sounds that he hoped would distract them enough to cause confusion and stop their progress. He accessed his considerable audio files, cobbling them together as best and quickly as he could. The idea was to lower speakers into the ocean and broadcast them well ahead of the island facility.

"Those chimera fish are slaughtering them," Ivan said.

It was true. The orcas may have tipped the scales in terms of numbers, but the ghost sharks had them beat on size and ferocity. The orcas must have sensed the ancient fish and gone for them, caught in the throes of their insatiable hunger. One or the other or both had demolished the underwater holding cage, setting up a bloody free for all.

The waters around the island were stained crimson. Ragged bits of orca bobbed on the waves.

Rosario said, "Maybe it can still work. We just need to lead the orcas away."

"And let them handle the rest," Raquel said, indicating the second, idling helicopter. It was loaded with Navy SEALs. Their job was to wipe out the chimera fish once and for all as soon as Chet and his team pulled the orcas clear of the island.

Chet's guts churned. "You've seen what happens. Once the orcas find a target, they don't stop until it's been obliterated. And those chimera fish aren't going to let a meal just walk away. They'll follow them."

"We have to at least try," Rosario said, tugging on his arm.

A giant chimera fish burst out of the water, two orcas flailing in its jaws. It clamped down on them, splitting their bodies in two before slamming back under the water.

"*Hijos de puta!*" Raquel screamed.

Chet didn't know what was worse, watching man slaughter the orcas with his weapons or a force of nature from millions of years ago savaging the majestic beasts. He got a chill thinking the ghost sharks were taking a certain degree of pleasure out of masticating the frenzied orcas.

"I just wish to hell they would do something about that Russian HAARP," he said, seething. "What the hell's taking them so long?"

"Don't count on it," Ivan said. He stalked along the edge of the roof with a scowl, watching the lunacy below. "You think it's easy to destroy something on Russian soil? They'll weigh the countermeasures Russia will take and back off. It will be easier for them if they wipe out every orca on the planet."

"Don't say that," Rosario said.

He looked at her with grim resolution. "Either way, someone loses. Us, or them. I think you know what they'll choose."

The door to the other helicopter swung open. A man who looked to be part mountain, clad in black, approached them. He held a formidable looking rifle against his chest, the barrel pointed at the ground.

"It appears we're late to the party," he said. He wore dark sunglasses, so Chet couldn't tell if he was talking directly to him.

"That doesn't mean we can't still try," Rosario said.

"Your call."

"Hey!"

Chet turned to see Ivan reach for Raquel and missing. She had found a ladder that led down the side of the building.

"Where is she going?" the SEAL asked.

Chet and Rosario ran over and saw Raquel scrambling down the rungs. She jumped off the last few, landing on her feet along the narrow strip of shoreline. Waves pounded the blood red sand and rocks. Hunks of flesh and blubber had washed ashore.

"Raquel, get back here!" Chet shouted.

"What do you think you're doing, you crazy bitch?" Ivan spat.

"Give me a gun," she said, eyeing the maelstrom that was dangerously close to her position.

The SEAL said, "I'll get her. If you want to try to lure those killer whales away from here, get in the chopper now."

"I'll stay with Raquel," Ivan assured Chet. "Someone has to make sure that impulsive lunatic doesn't get herself killed."

Chet had to peel himself away from the ledge with Rosario in hand. They ran into the helicopter, slamming the door shut.

He said to the pilot, "We're going to proceed as planned. Just take us a mile from the island and we'll deploy the speakers."

The pilot gave him a thumbs up, the engine humming to life.

Rosario handed him a helmet so they could hear each other when the chopper took to the sky.

"Raquel is out of her mind," Rosario said into the small microphone.

"I think we knew that when we rode in the car with her. We need to move the fight away from the island."

The helicopter lifted off. In seconds, they were above Raquel, Ivan and the SEAL, who was trying to push Raquel toward the ladder. Chet tensed when he saw her grab the man's pistol and run into the water. He couldn't hear anything, but he could see by the way her wrist kept jerking back that she was emptying the clip into the water. A gigantic chimera fish rose from the water, facing Raquel.

"I can't look," Rosario said.

It started to come for Raquel, just as the SEAL and Ivan had grabbed her from behind.

Suddenly, the chimera fish was slammed in its side by a trio of orcas, knocking it from its trajectory. It turned and ate the dorsal fin off one of the orcas. The other two dove under it before it could get them.

The scene faded as the chopper went further to sea.

"We're at the drop point," the pilot said.

Chet scrambled to the other door and slid it open. Rosario helped him lift the underwater speakers over the lip so they were dangling in the air. The speakers were attached to thick cables. Chet punched the button that lowered the speakers into the water.

Maybe he couldn't stop this pod from being demolished by the chimera fish, but he could divert the approaching pod from the melee. It was the longest of long shots, but there was literally nothing else to do.

Rosario fired up the laptop that contained the audio file. He clung to a hand bar on the side of the craft so he could be half-out of the chopper, making sure the speakers touched down. Once they disappeared under the water, he turned to Raquel and said, "Let 'er rip!"

He scrambled back to watch the display. They couldn't hear it, but a pulsating graphic showed them that sound was coming out of the speakers.

The water by the island was still a boiling frenzy of fighting. The ghost sharks were doing their best to devour every one of the orcas, but the pod was holding their own. Grabbing a pair of binoculars, Chet found it impossible to see if any of the ghost sharks were among the dead.

He did see that several other SEALs had made it to the shore. Their assault rifles were up and they were firing into the battle.

"No, not yet," Chet said.

"Not yet what?" Rosario asked, taking the binoculars. "Wait, it's okay. It looks like they're shooting a chimera fish that's riding on top of a row of orcas."

"Are they hitting the orcas?"

"I can't tell."

He looked at the display on the laptop, increasing the sound to the maximum level. "Are any orcas heading this way?"

"Um, I don't think so."

Chet tapped the pilot on the shoulder. "Maybe we should move in closer. They may not be able to hear it. With everything going on, it's probably deafening down there."

The chopper glided closer to the island, but slowly so as not to break the cables tethered to the speakers. Chet looked outside the door. He saw dozens of orcas still furiously engaged with the freed chimera fish. The speakers seemed to be doing nothing.

He could only imagine the frantic cries of the dying orcas, the living barking orders so they could somehow outflank the chimera fish. Generations of hunting tactics were useless against the behemoth ghost sharks. Unlike large whales when attacked by a pod of orcas, the ghost sharks were fast and vicious, ready to make any predator regret taking them on.

The recorded orca sounds emanating from the speakers might be as effective as spitting in a hurricane.

CHAPTER TWENTY-THREE

Jamel couldn't believe his eyes.

The power coming out of the Alaskan HAARP was off the charts. When he'd worked there, it wasn't capable of such force. The Navy, despite their cover story that they were done with HAARP, must have been very, very busy the past couple of years.

This was no mere test. They had turned that sucker on to do some damage.

And he knew exactly where it was focused.

In Kalach, the skies turned to coal, lightning illuminating the pitch. The ground shook as thunder that sounded as if it was issued from God himself pounded the atmosphere.

Hail the size of softballs pelted the hidden HAARP array, damaging the heavy-duty antennas. It came down with increasing ferocity, denting and twisting metal.

Windows shattered. The scientists in the main lab froze, knowing this was not nature bearing its weight upon them. Their computers flashed, then blinked out. Electricity was lost as jagged bolts of lightning rained down, striking up sparks. The smell of fried ozone stung their nostrils as they huddled in the center of the lab, careful not to get near the windows.

A call via landline was made to Moscow, reporting what had befallen the complex.

The floor of the lab bucked.

The bespectacled man dropped the phone, falling onto his side.

Now there was rumbling from below them as well. The ground shook and shattered, a rift opening up, spreading wider and wider until it swallowed the lab whole.

In Alaska, the men and women in charge of the HAARP facility were surrounded by the military. The readouts on their screens showed that the Kalach compound had been successfully destroyed. The intense storm had pounded Kalach both from above and below. Triggering the earthquake may have been heavy handed, but the powers that be had made it abundantly clear they didn't want anything left. Now all they had to do was wait for the satellite imagery to confirm that Russia's HAARP installation was nothing but a gaping crater filled with the shattered remains of their multi-billion dollar project.

"Kalach isn't the only one," someone said.

No, it wasn't. Now they would have to wait and see if they needed to redirect HAARP's attentions to another sector of the globe.

If anything, what happened here today was a kind of coming out party. Enemy nations were now put on notice that the most powerful weapon since the atomic bomb had not only been borne, but stepped confidently into adulthood.

"It's working!" Rosario shouted so loud, Chet almost ripped off his helmet. She was leaning out of the chopper and pointing.

"Finally, something's going our way." He then told the pilot to lead the orcas away from the island, but not fast enough for them to lose the audio in the going on under the surface.

The orcas were being trailed by the much larger chimera fish. Chet wasn't sure if the orcas were following the recording, or finally deciding to beat a hasty retreat from the slaughter.

"We have incoming," Chet said to Rosario.

The second chopper full of SEALs was in the air. They rained holy hell on the ghost sharks. The dinosaurs were just far enough behind the surviving orcas so they bore the full brunt of the assault. Side mounted machine guns tore into the chimera fish. Chet's mouth dropped open when there was a puff of smoke followed by some kind of missile that split a chimera fish in two as it exploded within its ancient flesh.

He spotted an inflatable boat in the water with several suicidal SEALs aboard. They were dumping something overboard, dangerously close to the remaining ghost sharks. The boat sped away just as two chimera fish broke the surface to swallow up the floating objects. They submerged quickly. The water swelled as whatever the SEALs had left for them detonated. A geyser of pink froth shot into the air.

Chet returned his attention to the orcas.

They were splitting up!

"Do a quick count and tell me how many you come up with."

He and Rosario did separate counts. It wasn't easy, but the pilot heard them and hovered over the dispersing pod as best as he could.

"I got fifty-six," Rosario said.

"I counted fifty-two. Close enough. Looks like they're splintering into their original pods."

Seven headed west, deeper into the Atlantic. A pod of twenty-one steered for Ireland's coast. The rest separated into two other pods, heading south. They no longer swam with the same mad urgency. It was almost as if nothing had happened, though Chet knew orca behavior enough to realize they would mourn the family they had lost.

"Can you take us back to the island?" he asked the pilot.

The reply came when the nose dipped and the chopper made a forty-five degree turn. They touched back down on the room minutes later. Ivan and Raquel sat by the ledge, soaked to the skin.

"Well?" Ivan asked.

"It looks like the orcas have returned to normal," Chet said. His legs felt like rubber, even though he wanted to pop some champagne.

"I shot one of those putas," Raquel said with a devilish smile.

"Yes, but he would have eaten you if those orcas hadn't saved your ass," Ivan reminded her.

"We look out for one another."

Rosario tugged on Chet's arm.

"Chet, what's that?"

He turned to see what had caught her attention.

His heart dropped to the floor.

After firing off the press release to all the media outlets he'd been able to find, Jamel thought it best to pack his shit up and get the hell out of Dodge. They would be on to him in a New York minute and he didn't want to stick around to find out what hole they'd dump him in for the rest of his life.

He'd blown everything wide open, from HAARP to Russia's involvement in the rash of orca attacks. He provided links and documents for them to fact check to their heart's content.

Sure, most of them would ignore his email. But it would only take a few. Once they picked up the story, the others would rush to follow suit. It may have sounded crazy, but Jamel was sure he'd given them enough facts to see past their disbelief. Besides, as he'd mused before, the world was a different place. The impossible was possible. Only those who willfully chose not to see were able to avoid the cold hard facts.

He struggled to carry several bags to his car. It was raining yet again. That would make driving difficult for him, as the roads out here weren't the best. Then again, it would be equally difficult for anyone coming to get him.

Jamel rushed back inside to make sure he had everything he needed. He hated leaving so much stuff behind, but there was only so much he could fit in his car and needed to be long gone before the men in black suits came for him.

A loud crash of thunder shook the floor, made everything on his shelves rattle and dance.

It can't be.

The weatherman had called for light rain today, but not a storm that felt like Thor's hammer pounding the heavens. Rain lashed the windows, pummeling the roof.

They weren't sending the men in the black suits this time around.

Stepping into the squall, Jamel looked to the pitch black sky, the cold, heavy rain blinding him. He'd lived through two hurricanes and one tornado, and none of them looked as foreboding as the pop up storm that had settled over his house.

Slamming the trunk closed, he was momentarily blinded by an intense flash of light.

Shielding his eyes, he leaned against the wet car to keep from falling.

"No," he whispered.

Seconds later, the light was followed by a deep, hideous rumble.

Jamel's tears intermingled with the cold, hard rain.

They were using HAARP to finish him, concentrating the array to build a super storm right over his head.

Live by the sword, die by the sword, he thought, seeing that there was no way he could drive out from under the black, roiling clouds. There just wouldn't be enough time. Not enough time to...

His keys slipped from his fingers, landing in a puddle.

There was no sense running now.

There wouldn't be anyplace to run to.

The flash of lightning hit him like a tractor beam, burning him to a crisp in seconds.

Chet held Rosario tightly in his arms as they watched a massive storm blossom from literally nowhere and head toward England's direction. Shards of lightning zigzagged within the onyx, gathering clouds. If there were such a thing as God's wrath from on high, this was it.

He couldn't believe what he was seeing. The storm swelled with each passing second, moving unnaturally fast, as if it were late for a date with death. It may have been a force of nature, but it was not nature that had culled it from the atmosphere.

"This can't be happening," Rosario sobbed.

Even from their safe vantage point, it was terrifying. Chet felt a primal fear seep into his bones. He wanted to look away, fall to his knees and pray. Pray that everyone and everything in the storm's path somehow managed to survive.

Chet had a feeling those prayers would not be answered.

Ivan cursed so long and loud, Chet could hear it over the whooshing of the helicopter's whirring blades. "Has everyone gone mad?"

Constant chatter bleated from the Navy helicopters. It was hard to make out exactly what was being said, but it appeared that intense weather activity had sprouted up all over Europe, North America and parts of Asia. Then the radios faded to static.

"They opened Pandora's box, and there's no closing the lid again," Chet said, feeling as if he'd been woken up from a nightmare only to tumble into a new, worse horror.

Jamel had been right. The military had taken out Russia's version of HAARP. Had they counted on other similar installations in Russia and their allies to counter attack? Who was to say that they could control the monstrous storms once they had been created? What they were witnessing looked far more terrifying and destructive than any nuclear blast. Mother Nature was an amoral, ruthless bitch, and they had just set her loose.

Chet watched a lingering orca, swimming amongst the remains of its fallen brethren, oblivious to the cataclysm occurring around them. It may have been looking for its mate or child. A vital part of it had been lost. He wondered how long orcas carried their grief. He hoped it wasn't forever.

They had somehow managed to save the orcas.

But at what cost?

THANK YOU!

This one is for my very special Hellions! So big props to the trio of Audra Stinson/Michael Fowler/Kimberly Yerina for being kick ass beta readers, Tim Feely (best horror fan any author can ask for), John Kilagon, Joachim Oliveira, Steven Gibson (I can always count on you, brother!), Steve Barnard (sorry, no zombie hookers in this one), Seth Crisp, Angela Lemieux (Ano!!!), William Drown, Pam Parish (high priestess of all things spooky), Jon Gauthier, Daniel Jervelius, Sean Stiff, Michael Patrick Hicks (that rare blend of awesome writer and reviewer), Chuck Buda (cuddle bear), Nick Zinn, Steve Tyndall, Frank Errington, Brian James Freeman and Tim Meyer (the man with horrible taste in horror movies).

Subscribe to the Dark Hunter Newsletter!
Become one of Hunter's Hellions and subscribe today to get your free story, special access to upcoming books and more!

http://tinyurl.com/h5fufn2

About the Author

Hunter Shea is the product of a misspent childhood watching scary movies, reading forbidden books and wishing Bigfoot would walk past his house. He doesn't just write about the paranormal – he actively seeks out the things that scare the hell out of people and experiences them for himself. Hunter's novels *The Montauk Monster* and *The Dover Demon* can even be found on display at the International Cryptozoology Museum. His video podcast, Monster Men, is one of the most watched horror podcasts in the world. He's a bestselling author of over 16 books, all of them written with the express desire to quicken heartbeats and make spines tingle. Living with his crazy and supportive family and two cats, he's happy to be close enough to New York City to see the skyline without having to pay New York rent. You can follow his travails at www.huntershea.com.

Look for these Severed Press titles from Hunter Shea

They Rise
Loch Ness Revenge
Savage Jungle : Lair of the Orang Pendek
Swamp Monster Massacre
Megalodon in Paradise

Coming in 2018:
The Dover Demon

SEVEREDPRESS

 facebook.com/severedpress
 twitter.com/severedpress

CHECK OUT OTHER GREAT
DEEP SEA THRILLERS

PREHISTORIC BEASTS AND WHERE TO FIGHT THEM
by Hugo Navikov

IN THE DEPTHS, SOMETHING WAITS ...

Acclaimed film director Jake Bentneus pilots a custom submersible to the bottom of Challenger Deep in the Pacific, the deepest point of any ocean of Earth. But something lurks at the hot hydrothermal vents, a creature—a dinosaur—too big to exist.

Gigadon.

It not only exists, but it follows him, hungrily, back to the surface. Later, a barely living Bentneus offers a $1 billion prize to anyone who can find and kill the monster. His best bet is renowned ichthyopaleontologist Sean Muir, who had predicted adapted dinosaurs lived at the bottom of the ocean.

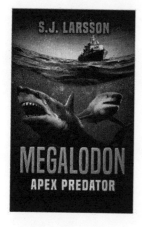

MEGALODON: APEX PREDATOR
by S.J. Larsson

English adventurer Sir Jeffery Mallory charters a ship for a top secret expedition to Antarctica. What starts out as a search and capture mission soon turns into a terrifying fight for survival as the crew come face to face with the fiercest ocean predator to have ever existed- Carcharodon Megalodon. Alone and with no hope of rescue the crew will need all their resources if they are to survive not only a 60 foot shark but also the harsh Antarctic conditions. Megalodon: Apex Predator is a deep-sea adventure filled with action, twists and savage prehistoric sharks.

facebook.com/severedpress
twitter.com/severedpress

CHECK OUT OTHER GREAT DEEP SEA THRILLERS

HELL'S TEETH
by Paul Mannering

In the cold South Pacific waters off the coast of New Zealand, a team of divers and scientists are preparing for three days in a specially designed habitat 1300 feet below the surface.

In this alien and savage world, the mysterious great white sharks gather to hunt and to breed.

When the dive team's only link to the surface is destroyed, they find themselves in a desperate battle for survival. With the air running out, and no hope of rescue, they must use their wits to survive against sharks, each other, and a terrifying nightmare of legend.

MONSTERS IN OUR WAKE
by J.H. Moncrieff

In the idyllic waters of the South Pacific lurks a dangerous and insatiable predator; a monster whose bloodlust and greed threatens the very survival of our planet...the oil industry. Thousands of miles from the nearest human settlement, deep on the ocean floor, ancient creatures have lived peacefully for millennia. But when an oil drill bursts through their lair, Nøkken attacks, damaging the drilling ship's engine and trapping the desperate crew. The longer the humans remain in Nøkken's territory, struggling to repair their ailing ship, the more confrontations occur between the two species. When the death toll rises, the crew turns on each other, and marine geologist Flora Duchovney realizes the scariest monsters aren't below the surface.

 SEVEREDPRESS

 facebook.com/severedpress
 twitter.com/severedpress

CHECK OUT OTHER GREAT
DEEP SEA THRILLERS

LOCH NESS REVENGE
by Hunter Shea

Deep in the murky waters of Loch Ness, the creature known as Nessie has returned. Twins Natalie and Austin McQueen watched in horror as their parents were devoured by the world's most infamous lake monster. Two decades later, it's their turn to hunt the legend. But what lurks in the Loch is not what they expected. Nessie is devouring everything in and around the Loch, and it's not alone. Hell has come to the Scottish Highlands. In a fierce battle between man and monster, the world may never be the same. Praise for THEY RISE : "Outrageous, balls to the wall...made me yearn for 3D glasses and a tub of popcorn, extra butter!" – The Eyes of Madness "A fast-paced, gore-heavy splatter fest of sharksploitation." The Werd "A rocket paced horror story. I enjoyed the hell out of this book." Shotgun Logic Reviews

TERROR FROM THE DEEP
by Alex Laybourne

When deep sea seismic activity cracks open a world hidden for millions of years, terrifying leviathans of the deep are unleashed to rampage off the coast of Mexico. Trapped on an island resort, MMA fighter Troy Deane leads a small group of survivors in the fight of their lives against pre-historic beasts long thought extinct. The terror from the deep has awoken, and it will take everything they have to conquer it.

36243369R00092

Made in the USA
Middletown, DE
12 February 2019